Alyssa Brugman attended five different schools in New South Wales, Australia and completed a business degree at Newcastle University. She began writing at age twenty-two.

Being Bindy is Alyssa's third published novel. Her first, *Finding Grace,* was shortlisted for a number of literary awards, including the Children's Book Council of the Year Award (Older Readers) and the New South Wales Premier's Award (Ethel Turner Prize). *Walking Naked,* her second novel, was published to critical acclaim.

She now lives in Sydney and works in public relations. Alyssa's website is: http://www.geocities.com/alyssabrugman

by the same author
Walking Naked

Being Bindy

Alyssa Brugman

ff

faber and faber

First published in 2005
by Faber and Faber Limited
3 Queen Square London WCLN 3AU

Published in Australia in 2004
by Allen and Unwin
83 Alexandra Street, Crows Nest
NSW, Australia

Printed in England by Bookmarque Ltd, Croydon
All rights reserved
© Alyssa Brugman, 2004

A CIP record for this book
is available from the British Library

ISBN 0–571–22705–8

2 4 6 8 10 9 7 5 3 1

My thanks to Layne, who listened without complaint from beginning to end, in 1000-word increments, and researched *Battlefield* 1942 for me with gusto. Many thanks also to Rosalind and Sarah for their continuing patience and perspicacity.

One

Every afternoon, except Wednesdays, my dad collected
me and Janey after school. She used to be fine with it,
but one day I noticed a change. It wasn't a big change –
just a little thing. When she got in the car, she slid down,
so no one could see her. My dad didn't care. He made a
joke of it, pretending we were spies.

'What news from the enemy?' he whispered, once
we'd slammed the doors.

'Janey's Going Out with Mitchell,' I replied. Even as
the words started coming out of my mouth, she gave me
a shut-up punch in the thigh.

'What?' I whispered. We always kept Dad up to date
with our love lives, even in Year 7 when we sometimes
had three different boyfriends in the space of a
lunchtime (none of whom we actually *spoke* to).

'Where are you going?' Dad asked.

Janey used to play along, but now she rolled her eyes
and sighed. 'We're not going anywhere.'

'So you're not going out with Mitchell?'

'No, I'm *Going Out* with him.'

1

'I thought you said you weren't going out with him.' Dad loved this game.

Then Janey mumbled, 'ISKWYML,' under her breath.

'What?' I asked.

'I'll tell you later.'

It turned out 'ISKWYML was code for *I so know why your mum left*. I tried to think of a code for Janey's mum, but she didn't embarrass us the way my dad did. She was happy to put us in a taxi, or let us out at some discreet location. Dad, on the other hand, always dropped us off in the middle of everyone and yelled out the window at the top of his lungs, 'Bye, girls!' accompanied by his daggy wave. My dad waves his hand up and down instead of from side to side.

The next day we were walking around the playground. I was trying to steer Janey away from the basketball court and towards the grassy mound outside B Block, where everyone sat around in circles talking and there were no fast-moving, head-sized balls flying around like heat-seeking missiles.

So far, Janey had never let us sit on the grassy mound, not even once, but I still suggested it every day because I knew I could wear Janey down eventually – even if it took years. Like when Janey got a *Chef Barbie* for her seventh birthday and she made me swap for *Totally Hair Barbie*. It was a trick because *Chef Barbie* sucked. It took me three years to make her swap back, but by then we didn't really play with them any more, and Janey had turned my *Totally Hair Barbie* into a Tibetan Monk.

Out of the blue, Janey said, 'Hey look, there's Hannah and the others,' as though it was something surprising, which it wasn't because they were sitting where they always sat – on the seats just behind the basketball court backboard.

So we headed over to them and Janey started chatting away. *What have you guys been doing? How did you go in that science test?* And then her bag just casually slipped off her shoulder onto the ground. Janey kept talking as though she hadn't noticed. *What are you picking for sport? Ice-skating? Really?*

Janey was talking, talking, and she bent down a little bit so she could hear what they were saying, and before too long they'd all shimmied up a little bit so she could sit down.

I was left standing at the edge of the court by myself, with my bag on my back, looking like a chump. Janey didn't even notice. She was too busy yakking it up about sport selections.

Next day at lunch, no perimeter preliminaries this time – after we'd been to the canteen, Janey marched straight down under the covered walkway to Hannah and the others, dropped her bag on top of the pile, and plonked down. I wasn't going to stand at the edge of the court again, but there was no room for me on the bench either. I ended up sitting cross-legged on the ground next to Janey as if I were her pet dog or something. So humiliating.

I didn't realise that this meant we were now *Sitting With* Hannah. I thought Janey didn't even *like* Hannah.

Janey used to say Hannah's skirt was too short, and that Hannah thought she was better than everyone else.

'You know, Janey didn't even buy a bag of chips at lunch. She bought a sausage roll. It was as though I didn't know her at all,' I complained to Dad that night over dinner.

'It's probably a good time to enlarge your group. You and Janey have been hanging around together since you were five years old,' he said. 'You've heard everything Janey' has to say.'

'But Janey is my best friend.'

'And she can still be your friend, but now you can have other friends too.'

'I don't want other friends. I work better as a half of a pair, not a third.'

Dad patted my arm. 'Maybe it's time to expand your horizons?'

Dad was big on Expanding Horizons. When Mum left, he started going to the gym, playing tennis, and doing Thai cooking and oil painting courses at the community centre. Only the Thai lasted, though. He used the oil painting that he'd done in class to cover the hole in the laundry ceiling.

Janey reckoned that he should get a better haircut instead of doing courses. I didn't like her bagging out my dad, but in this case, she was right. He had very bad hair.

It was long – not Long Hair, but like short hair that hadn't been cut. It was wiry and wispy with bits of grey and reddy-brown. It was a weird grey, too – an orangeygrey, like a red cattle dog. It looked as though he dyed it. Maybe he did? But I never saw him do it, and I never saw any empty dye bottles in the bin either. And if he *did* dye it, why would he dye it the same colour as a red cattle dog?

Anyway, on the whole Sitting With Hannah predicament, Dad wasn't much help.

There was no point talking to Mum about it either. She wasn't big on meaningful discussion. All her attention was on pretending she didn't have a new boyfriend. I thought about talking to Kyle about it, but when I knocked on his door, he didn't even look up from the computer screen. He said, 'What do you want, Spotty?'

'Can I talk to you?'

'No way, man. I'm pulling the best ping I've had all week.'

No, I was on my own.

Two

On Wednesday nights Janey's mum had her Craft Guild meeting. I usually stayed over because we could watch the movies Janey's mum didn't like us watching. She had a huge collection of those midday domestic-violence telemovies with names like, *To Dishonour and Abuse,* and *With this Ring I Thee Dread.* She thought they were too traumatising for us, but we thought they were funny. We spent most of the time yelling at the stupid heroines. 'Don't walk around backwards!' 'He's in the pantry!' 'Turn the lights on!'

After school, Janey's mum picked us up in her big real-estate sedan, and spent the whole drive home talking about her day. If she actually sold real estate it might have been a bit more exciting, but she was a property manager, so it was all blocked toilets and changing locks. One time, about four years earlier, a tenant had left a live python in the linen press, but most of the time they just left a mess and unpaid bills.

When we arrived, Hannah was sitting on the front step. At her feet was a big sports bag stuffed full, as if she was staying for a week. I was surprised. Janey hadn't said anything about Hannah coming over.

Janey's mum gave Hannah a little wave. She pressed the grey remote on her dashboard and the garage door jerked slowly upwards.

'What time do you girls want to go?' Janey's mum asked.

Janey shrugged. 'About 7.30.'

Her mother nodded. 'Order yourselves a cab,' she said. 'I can pick you up on the way back. You text me when you're ready, OK?'

Janet' gave her a quick peck on the cheek and we jumped out.

'Ready to go where?' I asked, watching Janey's mum back out of the driveway.

'I thought maybe we could go to the movies,' Janey said, walking towards the garage.

'But I've only brought my jammies,' I said.

'You can borrow something of Hannah's.'

Hannah slipped under the garage door, waited for us to move inside and then pressed the control on the wall *without even looking*. She must have been to Janey's place lots of times.

Inside Janey's room, Hannah started unpacking her bag – pulling out tops, jeans, skirts and laying them out on the bed, or holding them against herself and looking in the mirror. Janey reached into her cupboard and pulled out about five different pairs of shoes that I'd never seen before.

'What about the little cream top?' Janey asked.

Hannah flicked me a glance. 'I was thinking about the off-the-shoulder one.'

'SVC,' Janey said, standing back with her hands on her hips.

'SVC?' I asked.

'So very chic,' Hannah replied.

There was a pause.

'WWTA?' I asked.

'Sorry?' asked Hannah.

'What's with the acronyms?' I replied.

Hannah looked at Janey and curled her lip.

Janey ignored both of us. 'These shoes will fit her.'

Hannah nodded. 'Why don't you just pop in the shower?' she said to me. 'You'll need to wash your hair. There are towels under the . . .'

'I *know* where the towels are. I *have* been here before, you know,' I snapped.

'OK,' Hannah replied. 'No need to chuck a wobbler.'

'What's going on, Janey?' I asked.

Hannah and Janey exchanged a glance. 'We're just going to the movies,' Janey said.

'We want you to look nice. That's all. No biggie,' added Hannah.

'It will be fun,' said Janey, smiling. Then she looked at her watch. 'We've only got about an hour and we need showers too, so try not to be too long, okies?'

After my shower I put my bra and undies on, wrapped the towel around myself and went back to Janey's room.

I could hear her talking to Hannah as I came down the hallway.

'Did you really say that?' asked Janey.

'Nah, I just told her it was a couples thing. Poor Cara. She has no clue.'

'SHNC,' said Janey, and they both giggled.

I stepped inside the room and they both shut up. Hannah disappeared out the door and into the bathroom.

They'd laid out an outfit for me on the bed.

'What's this?' I asked, holding up a little slip of black material.

'That's your top. Hannah got it in Hong Kong. They don't sell them here,' Janey told me, slipping it over my head.

I turned to look at myself in the mirror. 'You can see my bra.'

'So? Take it off. What's the matter with you? You've got a nice pair of boobs,' she said, and to my horror, she cupped her hand around one of them.

'Janey! What are you doing?' I pushed her away.

'Stop being so dumb. It's just a boob. We've all got them. Here, put this skirt on.'

She held up a skirt that was about 30 centimetres long.

'I thought that was a belt!'

'Ha de ha ha,' she replied, and she pulled my towel off.

'Janey!'

'What? You've got undies on,' she said, handing me the skirt. 'I've seen you in swimmers – it's just the same.'

I bent down and buttoned up the skirt. Janey started strapping a pair of shoes to my feet. Then she stood up and turned me towards the mirror.

9

'There, see?' she said.

Hannah and I were roughly the same size and proportion, so I couldn't understand why her clothes seemed at least two sizes too small.

'I can't wear these. I'll fall over. Can't I wear my own shoes?' I asked, looking down at my feet.

'Your shoes don't go with this skirt, silly,' she said. Then she skipped down the hallway to the bathroom.

Hannah came in with a towel around her hair and slipped into a top that looked very much like a hanky. She reached into her big bag again, took out a huge make-up kit and unfolded it over Janey's desk.

She took me by the shoulders and steered me towards the chair. I sat down and she stood with one leg on either side of mine – invading my space. I leaned back in the chair as far as I could.

'I don't need any make-up,' I said.

'Yes, you do,' she replied. 'It'll bring out your eyes.'

'I prefer them in my head,' I replied.

Nothing from Hannah, not even a smile. She took out a bottle of foundation, squirted it into her hands and rubbed her palms together. 'A little bit for you,' she said, massaging it on my cheeks. 'And a little bit for me.' She smeared the rest across her own face.

'Now, close your eyes,' she said.

I could feel Hannah's little brush and pencil, first on one eye and then the other. Her breath blew on my cheek. It was weird having her right there in my face – uncomfortable.

'Open. Just a little bit of mascara, and then you're done,' she said.

I tried to hold my eyes open, but they were watering.

'Stop doing that. You'll make it run, and then we'll have to start all over again,' she complained.

I mumbled, 'I'm not doing it on purpose,' and tried not to breathe in her breath.

'There,' she said and stood back, smiling.

Janey was standing in the doorway. 'Look at you!'

'Let me see,' I said and started to stand up.

'Not yet,' said Hannah, pushing me down again. She picked up a hairbrush and the dryer and started pulling at my hair, working her way from the bottom to the top of my head. I wished she would stop touching me. It was kind of intimidating.

'That hurts,' I complained.

'Pain is beauty,' Hannah replied.

Janey got dressed in a sparkly bustier, hot pants and a long crochet jacket over the top. She started covering her eyelids with shiny eyeshadow.

'What do you think?' she said, turning around.

'Oh yes, very J Lo,' said Hannah. 'I'm finished here.'

I turned to look at myself in the mirror and let out a little gasp. Hannah had coated my eyes in black. My hair was all booted up and knotty. It looked as if I'd been in a fight – and lost – badly.

Janey said, 'You look just like Christina Aguilera.'

'I look like a slut,' I said.

Hannah rolled her eyes. 'Geez, Belinda, we're doing you a favour. Will you stop bitching?'

'Janey, I can't go out like this. And you shouldn't be going out like *that*,' I said, looking her up and down.

'I think I look nice,' she said, lifting her chin.

'This whole outfit,' I said, looking down at the clothes I was wearing, 'it's not *me*, Janey. And that's not you, either. It might be Hannah, but it's not us.'

'Then maybe what you need is a personality transplant,' Hannah said, putting her hands on her hips.

'I wasn't talking to you,' I said, turning to her.

'And a good thing too. Because if you were talking to me, I might have to smack you in the face.'

'Just cut it out will you? Both?' said Janey. She took me by the shoulders and sat me down on the edge of the bed. 'Look, Bindy, we could have taken Cara, or any of the others out with us tonight, but we picked you. Any one of them would love to borrow Hannah's clothes and have Hannah do their hair.'

'Why didn't you pick one of the others, then?' I asked.

'Because I want *you* to come with me. I want you to look nice.' She smiled at me. 'You don't have to be average any more.'

Three

I tried to get in the taxi without giving the cabby a chance to see up my skirt, but he looked anyway. He looked down Hannah's top too, and as for Janey, she didn't have much of a top to look down, so he had a great big gawk at her without even straining.

I sat in the back and after a while the lack of airflow and strong smell of hair products made me woozy. I started to roll down the window but Hannah went nuts, saying that I was going to ruin her hairstyle, even though she was sitting in the front. I left it open a fraction and sat up as straight as I could, trying to get my face closer to the gap.

When we got out at the Mall, the cabby gave us a grin and a wink. 'Need a cab home, do youse? Wanna take my card? I'll pick you up again, no sweat.'

Then Hannah – I couldn't believe it – she smiled at him, took his card and shoved it in the top of her pants. After he drove away, she threw the card on the ground and Janey laughed.

We walked past the shops – Janey and Hannah in

front, and me straggling behind. There was a wind blowing on my skin where there shouldn't have been a wind. I tried to pull my skirt down a little bit as I took the escalator up to the cinema complex.

Outside the theatre there was a group of people loitering. Some of the boys were from school. Most of the guys looked us up and down – even the ones with girlfriends on their arms. The girls looked at us too.

I wanted to slip past them as quickly and quietly as possible, but Hannah and Janey headed straight towards them, smiling and bouncing, as if they were in a shampoo ad.

Next thing you know, three guys separated themselves from the larger group – Mitchell, Lucas, who was Hannah's current boyfriend, and another boy called James. He was in my Science and English classes.

James is quite good-looking. He has dark brown hair and a sprinkling of freckles across his nose. He's also a little bit strange. He carries his schoolbooks around in a plastic shopping bag.

The other four paired off and James walked towards me. Ahh, so this was the 'couples thing' Hannah had been talking about.

'Hi, er, Belinda. You look nice tonight,' he said, flicking his eyes down to my boobs and up again.

I folded my arms across my chest. 'Sorry,' he said, looking ashamed.

He put his arm around my waist and I jumped.

'Oops,' he said, holding his hands up.

The others were already in the line for tickets. Janey

grabbed my arm and pulled me along the queue to where she was standing. An older couple, standing behind her, frowned.

'She's with us. She's got frontage,' Janey explained.

'I can see that,' said the man, and his girlfriend slapped him on the arm.

I felt the colour rise in my cheeks. 'You never said anything about this being a date,' I whispered to Janey in a hissy voice, sounding just like my mother.

'Surprise!' she said, and she laughed. Mitchell slobbered on her neck.

'Janey!' I said.

'What?' she asked, smiling as though she *liked* it.

James pushed in next to me, apologising to the older couple. When we got to the front of the queue, James bought tickets for both of us.

'I didn't bring any money. I didn't know about any of this,' I explained. 'I'll pay you back tomorrow.'

'Don't worry about it. Maybe you can make it up to me somehow.' He winked, and then laughed nervously.

I wrinkled my nose. James blushed deeply. 'Do you want a drink or something?' he mumbled.

'Thanks. Maybe just a Coke.'

We stood in silence, taking one painfully slow step after the other towards the food counter. After James bought our drinks we followed the others into the cinema. Mitchell, Janey, Hannah and Lucas sat in a row in the middle. About five rows behind them were the rest of the basketballers.

James herded me up the stairs towards them. When

we got to the row I stopped, but James wasn't watching me, he was waving to the other guys, and he ran into me, spilling my drink.

'You're smooth, Jimmy,' one of them called out.

James ignored them as best he could. 'Oops! Sorry. Do you want me to buy you another one?'

'No, that's fine.'

James walked sideways along the row and plonked down next to Lucas. I sat down next to him, feeling my skirt sliding up. I would have to remember to stand up before the lights came on or I would give the people behind me a great view of my bum.

James tried for conversation. 'So, do you like movies?'

'It depends on the movie,' I replied.

'Yeah, it does, doesn't it?' he said.

After a moment, he asked, 'What's your favourite movie then?'

'What? Ever?'

'Yeah.'

'I don't know. Talk about putting me on the spot. What's your favourite movie?'

'Did you like that *American Pie*?' he asked.

I looked down at my lap. 'Actually, that's the only movie I have ever walked out of.'

'Oh,' he said. 'It was pretty dumb, eh?'

'Well, as much as I saw of it, yeah.'

The lights started to dim. *Thank God*.

A couple moving up the stairs quickened their pace in order to get into their seats before it was completely dark. They stopped two rows in front of ours. The woman decided to slide along the row with her back to the screen. I could see her face. Why couldn't she have faced the other way? Why couldn't she have arrived two minutes later, when it was dark? Why couldn't she have chosen a different movie theatre? A different movie? Or hired a video that night?

Just at the last minute as she was about to turn around – at the very same moment that James decided to slide his arm around my shoulders – she looked up and her eyes caught mine. Only two rows between us there was no possibility that we had mistaken each other for someone else.

I switched my eyes from her to the man she was with. He was taller than I had imagined, and younger, too.

I looked back at her again. She was still standing there with her mouth open. The whole incident must have taken only a split second but the man knew something was wrong. 'Darling, what's the matter?' he asked.

She didn't say anything. She just closed her mouth, swivelled around and sat down.

There we were, my mother and I, not five metres apart for the next *two hours* – each of us knowing that at some stage we would have to get up and leave.

Four

Actually, it didn't end up being that bad. I expected her to drag me out of there, or at least do *something*. Dad would have. If he'd caught me dressed that way, he would have given everybody there a stern talking-to. Then he would have taken down all their names and phone numbers and given their parents a stern talking-to as well. Mum didn't even turn around. As soon as the credits started to roll, she was up and out of there.

The first wave of basketballers bounded down the steps behind her and nearly bowled her over. 'Watch it!' I heard her hiss at one of them. James stood up too, as did Janey and Co. I sat tight.

'What's the hold-up?' Janey said.

I pointed towards the stairs.

'Who is it, Bindy?' she said loudly.

'Shhh!' I said and covered my face with my hands. As if that was going to help.

'What?' she whispered back, but by then Mum was gone.

'Nothing. It doesn't matter,' I said. I forgot to pull my

skirt down and gave the second wave of basketballers a thrill.

'Look at that!' one of them yelled.

I tugged at the hem, feeling the blood rush to my face. James rolled his eyes. 'They're boys. Just ignore them.'

'I don't care,' I said. 'I just want to go home.'

Without waiting for the others, I walked downstairs, across the foyer and out the front door. I moved over to the edge of the terrace and rubbed my arms against the cold.

After a minute or two, James walked up behind me. 'The other guys have gone in to play the pinnies,' he said. 'Do you want to play too?'

'Where's Janey?' I asked.

'Down there,' he said, pointing to the food court below. It was dark, and all the shop shutters were down. Janey and Mitchell were sitting at a table in the court-yard with their arms around each other, kissing. Hannah was not far away leaning against a wall with Lucas pressed against her. It was yuck. They looked like a pair of cheap tarts.

I turned away. James stood directly in front of me. He leaned forward – his face close to mine.

'What are you doing?' I asked.

'I was going to . . . you know, kiss you.'

'Well, don't,' I said, taking a step to one side.

He took a little step sideways so that he was directly in front of me again. 'Will you Go Out with me, Belinda?' He leaned forward again.

'Stop it!' I said.

'What?' he asked. 'What am I doing wrong? I bought you a Coke and that.'

'I don't even *know* you, James, and the only thing you know about me is that I didn't like *American Pie*. And you did! So what have we got in common?'

'It's not like we have to get married,' he replied.

'Well, what is it like?'

'I don't know. We could have a kiss. You might enjoy it. And then we can find out things we have in common after.'

'And what if we still don't have anything in common?'

He shrugged. 'If we're kissing, then we don't have to talk.'

I started walking towards the cinema foyer. 'Where are you going?'

'I'm going to ring my dad. I want to go home.' Then I stopped in my tracks. I didn't have any money.

James tapped me on the shoulder. 'Want to use this?' He was holding out his mobile.

'Thanks.'

I quickly dialled my number and pressed Send. 'Ya-ello,' came Dad's voice.

'Dad?'

'Hey there, kiddo, what's up?'

'I'm at the Mall. I need you to come and get me. It's been a very bad night.'

'What are you doing there? Where's Janey?' he asked. 'She's . . .' *Expanding her horizons.* 'Janey's with Hannah and a few others. She's not coming home with us. Can you come and get me? Soon?'

'Done,' he said.

'And Dad? Promise not to freak out when you see me? I'm just warning you in advance. I want you to know that it wasn't my idea.'

'Hmmm,' he said. 'OK. I'll put my best unfreaked face on. Bindy, are you safe?'

'Yes.'

I handed the phone back to James. 'Thanks.'

'Do you want me to wait with you?' he asked, slipping it into his pocket.

'It's probably best if I wait by myself. My dad might think . . .'

James nodded. 'Yeah, I know what I'd think. I *did* think. But I'm not going to let you wait on your own. Someone might stop and try to pick you up, if you know what I mean. I'm not much protection, but I'm better than nothing.'

'I suppose.' I shrugged.

We walked down the escalator, across the food court and down the stairs to the street. James stood next to me with his hands in his pockets, scuffing his feet on the footpath.

I felt really stupid standing there and not talking, so I tried to think of a topic. 'Why do you carry your books in a shopping bag?' I asked.

'Because if I don't, then the bags just get thrown away.'

'So?'

He shrugged. 'It seems like a waste to buy another bag when there are shopping bags just lying around.'

'But don't they break?'

James nodded. 'Then I use another one.'

When he put it like that, it didn't seem all that strange.

More awkward silence. James pulled out his phone and started tossing it from hand to hand, but then, after a particularly vigorous fling, it clattered to the ground. He picked it up, slipped it back in his pocket and pretended to be really interested in the parked cars along the street. Who knows? Maybe he really was interested?

'So, what do you like doing?' I asked.

'Well, basketball. But I like to read sometimes, too.'

'What do you read?' I asked.

'Mostly fantasy or sci fi.'

'Are you hard-core, like Asimov, or Arthur C. Clarke?' I asked.

James grinned. 'See? We do have something in common. Will you kiss me now?'

I shook my head.

'All right, but you owe me a movie,' he said, pointing at me. 'And a phone call. And a Coke.'

Shortly after that, Dad pulled up. He wound down the window on the passenger side. 'It *is* you.'

'Hi, Dad. This is James.'

'Hello, young man.'

James leaned down and offered his hand to Dad. 'I just want you to know, sir, I didn't do anything to your daughter.'

'That's good, James. That's very good,' he replied, shaking James's hand. He looked at me, his smile quickly disappearing. 'Get in.'

He pulled out into the road. I could tell he was cross. 'Why didn't you tell me where you were?'

'I didn't even know!' I protested.

'You should have rung straight away. When you change plans, then you let me know – that's the rule, kiddo.'

While I was in the shower washing all the make-up off my face, he phoned Janey's mum to tell her that I was home safe and sound. She didn't even know that I was supposed to be there. Janey had already told her some story about how I'd got a lift home with one of the others.

I didn't tell Dad about seeing Mum. Both of them seemed to have rewritten their life scripts as though the other never existed.

It had been a very bad night – a 'VBN', as my New and Improved best friend might have said.

Five

The next day we had sport selections. Hannah and the other girls had managed to get a spot at the front of the queue. You had to be quick if you wanted something decent. Janey and I were dawdling. We'd never cared about which sport we did.

When we first arrived at High School we did swimming. We couldn't understand why nobody else had chosen it until the temperature started to drop. After that I pretended to have an ear infection every sports day and Janey strapped on her old cast from when I broke her arm in third class. It didn't fit any more but, bandaged up, you couldn't see the split.

In the second half of Year 7 we chose hockey. Our school had quite a strong hockey team, so Janey decided that all we had to do was to suck at hockey (that was easy) and they would put us on the bench, where we could play noughts and crosses. We kept score, and at the end of the season I was winning 512 to 426.

I didn't expect this time to be any different, so I was surprised when we headed over to the table marked

'Ice-skating' – which everyone wanted to do. The teacher said, 'Sorry, girls, we're full up here.'

Janey ran her finger down the page, and there was *Jane Madden* right underneath Hannah Plummer on the list.

I scanned, scanned – no Belinda Grubb. 'Can you fit one more in?' I asked.

The teacher shook her head. 'Sorry. There are still some places in ping-pong or yoga.'

Ping-pong? I didn't even know they offered ping-pong. What next? Totem tennis?

'We can do yoga, I suppose,' I said, turning away. 'At least it's close to home so Dad won't have to come and pick us up.'

Janey didn't say anything. I thought she was still cross about me leaving the mall early. When I'd arrived that morning, she and Hannah were waiting for me with their arms folded.

'You didn't even say goodbye or anything. We had to make up something to cover for you,' Janey' said.

'That's so rude,' added Hannah. 'Where are my clothes, anyway? You've got about a hundred bucks' worth of my stuff, you know. You'd better bring it tomorrow.'

'I don't want your clothes, Hannah,' I replied. Since then, Janey' had barely said two words to me.

Off we went to line up for yoga. Janey stood there with a grim expression on her face. When we got to the head of the queue I wrote my name in neat letters and handed Janey the pen.

She didn't take it from me. 'What are you doing?' I said.

She looked at a spot on the wall behind my head. 'I think I might stay in ice-skating.'

'But there aren't enough spaces,' I said.

'Maybe someone will drop out and you can move over later?' she offered.

'Who drops out of sport? It's compulsory!'

'Maybe someone will break their leg or something?' She shrugged.

I stared at her. 'Milk Pig!'

'Milk Pig' was an expression that started one time when Dad took us camping. Kyle, Janey and I had a big fight because somebody got up in the middle of the night and drank all the milk and there was none left for cereal. We knew *somebody* had done it, because in the bin was the empty milk container ringed with Milo. Not only had the culprit drunk all the milk — and we're talking over a litre — but straight from the container too. The argument went round and round in circles about who was the 'Milk Pig'. Ever since then the 'Milk Pig' was somebody who didn't think about anybody else — somebody selfish.

'Is this because I beat you at noughts and crosses?' I asked. 'Because we can change it to boxes if you like, or hangman. And what about a lift home? You can't expect Dad to make the trip just to pick you up.'

She flicked her hair over her shoulder. 'I'll get a lift home with someone else,' she said, and we walked over to Hannah and the others. I didn't sit down. I stood at the edge of the group, irritated. I saw James over the other side of the hall and he waved.

'What'd she end up with?' I heard Hannah ask Janey in a whisper.

'Yoga,' she mumbled. So it was all planned.

Hannah smiled at me sweetly. 'You know, I heard that Cameron Diaz does yoga – and Gwyneth Paltrow.'

'Oh really?' I snapped. 'I didn't see their names on the list.'

I stood with my back to them. James wandered towards me scrabbling around inside his shopping bag. He grinned at me and pulled out a book. 'Hello again. I brought you this. It's my favourite book in the whole world, so I'm not giving it to you, but you can borrow it.'

The Magician. Dad had read it to us years ago, but I decided not to disappoint James by telling him.

'I'd better look after it, then,' I said, running my finger along its worn spine. 'Thanks, James.'

He pushed his hands deep in his pockets and twisted back and forth so that his bag swung around his knees. 'Can I tell you something?'

'I suppose so,' I said.

He took me by the elbow and edged away so the others couldn't hear.

'I'm sorry about how I was last night. It's just that . . . He looked over his shoulder. He twisted faster and faster, his bag banging briskly against his legs. 'I've started to . . . think about girls a fair bit. OK, a lot. I think it might be hormones.'

He gave me a furtive little glance and then stared fiercely at his shoes. 'I don't know what to say to them. I just say stupid stuff and sound like an idiot. I don't think I'm ever going to talk one into . . . doing stuff with me.'

'And?' I prompted.

He lifted his bag up and started winding it tightly around his wrist. 'Last night, once we got talking it was fine, but maybe you could . . . you know, tell me what I'm supposed to say, or at least tell me when I've said something dumb.'

I hesitated. 'I suppose I could do that.'

He gave me another quick glance and continued, 'For example, I've been standing over there watching you and imagining what you might look like in swimmers. Can I tell you stuff like that? I mean, should I?'

I blushed and looked away. 'Probably not.'

He paused, holding his bag out in front of him and letting it spiral loose. 'Want to go swimming with me?'

'No thanks, James.'

'Oh.'

We both stood there, faces as red as tomatoes, not looking at each other.

'So . . . are we still friends?' he asked.

'Yes, James.'

He nodded. 'Good. Well. See ya.' Then he turned around, threw his bag over his shoulder and sauntered back to his friends.

Six

At least I had Janey to myself after school . . . or so I thought.

Janey had been coming over to my house ever since kindy. My dad runs a panel-beating business from a workshop at the back of our house, so he's there all the time. Most days, Janey's mum didn't get home from work until six, and she collected Janey from our place on the way.

Janey's mum is a proper mother. She bakes. She makes mega Anzac cookies, almond slice and fudge. She used to drop in a box of home-baked goodies to our place at least once a week and have coffee with Dad.

When we were little, Dad used to make us sprinkle sandwiches and a glass of milk, and plonk us in front of the cartoons. Then he would go back to the workshop. There was an intercom in the kitchen to call him, if we wanted anything.

When we were really small, we couldn't quite reach the buzzer, so Dad made us a step out of an old wheel arch. One time in third class, Janey was annoying me, so

I banged her over the head with the television remote. As she climbed up to press the buzzer, I pulled the step away from under her. That's how she broke her arm.

Once we got into high school, we were old enough to look after ourselves but Janey came over anyway. We didn't have sprinkle sandwiches any more; we had noodles, or crackers with cheese.

The afternoon of the Sport Selections Incident, we settled down in front of the cartoons and had something to eat, the way we always did – then Janey took the remote and changed it to MTV.

'Come on, let's dance,' she said. Then she got up and started gyrating and thrusting her hips the way they did on the television.

Ages ago, when we did tap, we used to put on a CD and make up a dance together, but it always told a story, say for example, we'd be two elves who were lost, or a pair of cats or something. There was never any thrusting.

'We're missing *Dexter's Laboratory*,' I said, picking up the remote and switching it back.

Janey flopped back on the lounge. 'You're such a stickin-the-mud, Bindy.'

She jiggled her leg, hummed, and picked at her fingernails. I ignored her, cupping my hands to either side of my face like horse blinkers, and the next thing you know, it was time for *Top Cat* and she was gone.

I thought she'd gone to the loo, but by the end of *Top Cat* and well into *Looney Tunes* she was still missing. I investigated. She wasn't in the kitchen, or in my room, or out the back. I even went into Dad's workshop. No Janey.

Eventually I found her in the very last place I would ever check. In fact, it was so unlikely that I didn't even look. I only discovered her there because I heard her giggling from inside. Janey was in Kyle's room.

I opened the door and there they were in the dark, hunched over Kyle's computer. *We've got 'em on the run,* said the PC.

'Hello, Snot-face,' Kyle said looking up.

'What are you doing?' I asked.

'We're fighting the Battle of the Bulge,' Janey replied. She had the controls and didn't look up from the monitor.

'Look there,' said Kyle, pointing at the screen. 'There's a guy with a pineapple.'

'A what?' asked Janey.

'A hand-grenade. *Run! Run!* Ooooh, you killed my little guy! What were you doing?'

'I didn't see it!' she said.

'Doesn't matter. You can re-spawn over there,' he replied. Then he looked up at me again. 'Are you going out or coming in?'

'What?' I asked.

'You're in the doorway. You can't stand there,' he said. 'It makes a glare on the screen and little people die.' Then he turned back to Janey. 'You know, guns don't kill people, glare kills people.'

Janey thought he was hilarious.

There was only *The Jetsons* on, which was quite boring, so I thought I might watch the Battle of the Bulge for a while. I sat on the edge of Kyle's bed and watched him teach Janey how to throw pineapples until her mum tooted for her.

The next afternoon she didn't even pretend to watch cartoons with me. She marched straight into the kitchen, made two serves of macaroni and cheese, and instead of heading for the lounge-room, she turned up the hallway.

'Are you coming?' she asked, standing outside Kyle's door.

I hesitated, then I followed her up the hall, but when I got to the door I saw her hand one of the bowls (*my* bowl) to Kyle!

'Milk Pig!'

'Am not!' she protested through a mouthful. 'There's a whole 'nother packet in the cupboard. You've got arms and legs.'

I frowned and went back to the lounge-room to watch *Dexter's Laboratory*.

And that's how it went from then on. After school Janey went straight into Kyle's room and I joined them after *Top Cat*. I tried to get interested in the game, but after a while I just lay on Kyle's bed reading James's book, trying not to be infuriated by their yelling and hooting, and how the two of them having such a wonderful time made me feel like a great big useless third.

Seven

I shouldn't have been surprised when Janey turned up at my house on a second Saturday. I answered the door, and there she was standing on the doorstep. Her hair was in loose curls and she had make-up on. She must have been practising, because, the last time I saw her do her own make-up, she looked as though she'd been smacked in the face with a couple of paintballs.

'I'm going to Mum's,' I said.

'I know,' she replied, pushing past me into the hallway.

'What are you doing here?'

'I'm going out with Kyle,' she said.

'You're Going Out with Kyle?'

'No, silly,' she said, rolling her eyes, 'We're going to a LAN – to play *Battlefield.*'

'Oh,' I replied. Kyle had never asked *me* to go to a LAN.

Dad emerged from the kitchen. 'Janey!' He grabbed her in a headlock and ruffled the hair on the top of her head with his knuckles, the way he always did.

'Stop it! You're ruining my hair!'

'Sorreeh!' he said, letting her go. Janey sniffed and marched down the hallway to Kyle's room. Dad looked at me with a surprised expression on his face, as if to say, *What's wrong with her?*

'No idea,' I replied.

Kyle and Janey left for their LAN, and as they reached the door Kyle turned around. 'Be careful, Bindy.' He always said that. I don't know why he'd turned into such a worrywart.

After the Cinema Incident, I was *sooo* not looking forward to seeing Mum. I thought about telling her I couldn't go because I had something contagious – perhaps Ebola – but instead I just waited and hoped that she'd forget to come and get me, or maybe forget she had a daughter altogether.

When she pulled up in her zippy little sports car and grinned at me, I guessed that we were pretending that the whole movie business never happened. That suited me just fine.

'What would you like to do this weekend, chicken?'

I don't know why she bothered asking. She always had activities planned out in advance. They would be really cool things to do too – if I was going with Janey; if I didn't have to do it with just Mum, but Mum wouldn't let me bring Janey. She said she wanted to be able to concentrate on *me,* but what she meant was, she wanted all my attention on *her.*

'I don't mind, Mum, whatever you want to do.'

'I thought we could go to Wonderland,' she said. I grunted.

'Wouldn't Wonderland be fun? Afterwards we could go up to the Blue Mountains. They have all those great old guest-houses. We'll have a nice dinner and sleep over. Then tomorrow we can do some shopping, if you like.' She turned her head away from me as she pulled the car out into the traffic.

'Whatever.'

'Won't that be nice?' she asked.

'I'm sure *you* will have a great time,' I grumbled.

Mum didn't say anything for a minute or two, she just drove. Then she pulled over to the side of the road and folded her arms. She spoke to me in her fast, hissy voice. She used to use it on my father. I always thought it was because she didn't want us to hear what they were arguing about, but now I know it's just what she sounds like when she's really cranky.

'I've gone to quite a bit of effort to plan a nice weekend with you, but we're not really getting off to a very good start, are we? I certainly don't intend to take you if you are going to be . . . *adolescent*.'

I am adolescent, I thought, but I didn't say it. No way. Not when she was going off.

'Do I have to turn this car around and take you back to your father's? Because I will – don't you think that I won't.' I sat there looking at my hands in my lap.

'*Well?*'

'No, Mum. We'll go to Wonderland and then we'll go up to the mountains.'

'What do you say?'

'Thank you?'

'And what else? Hmm?'

I didn't know what she was after, so I shrugged.

'An apology would be nice,' she prompted.

'Sorry, Mum,' I mumbled.

'That's better. Now put a smile on that face.'

At Wonderland we went on nearly every ride. Mum squealed and laughed. When we went on the Snowy River Rampage, Mum took off her safety belt and leaned over the side, reaching towards the water. You weren't supposed to do that. The sign said you had to keep-inside-the-carriage-at-all-times. 'This water is icy,' she said. 'Feel it.'

I folded my arms. There was no way I was going to lose a limb over some dumb water.

'Isn't this fun?'

'Yes, Mum,' I replied with a big fake smile. *Oh yeah, this is choice.* I tried my best not to be . . . adolescent.

She made a big furry Barney Rubble take a photo of us, and just before he took it, she squeezed my shoulder – hard. *Smile!* I was going to have fun if she had to beat it out of me.

Afterwards we drove up to the mountains. It was just on dusk by then. Mum wound down all the windows and inhaled with gusto. 'Smell that fresh air! Isn't it glorious. Take a deep breath, chicken.'

I breathed through my chattering teeth. My jumper was in the boot and Mum wouldn't stop to let me get it out. I was *so* glad when we stopped at the guest-house in Katoomba.

'Isn't this lovely?'

It had been built in the 1920s. It had a tall, green pitched roof and chunky brick chimneys, and was circled with wide verandahs. Inside were vast hallways, richly carpeted. It could have come straight from the set of *The Shining*. Who knows? Maybe it was?

Red Rum.

Dinner was OK, if you're into slabs of meat and overcooked veggies. The conversation was pretty predictable.

'How's school?'

'Good.'

'Are you getting good marks?'

'Yes.'

'What's your favourite subject?'

Pick a subject, any subject. It wasn't as if she was going to know the difference.

'Science.'

'Really? See, you *do* take after me.'

Silence.

'Kyle's more like your father.'

Longer silence.

Kyle stopped coming to see her ages ago – around the time he stopped calling her 'Mum' and started calling her 'Adele'.

'Tell me about Kyle. Has he got a girlfriend? How is he doing at school? Is he playing any sport?'

I thought it might be an idea for her to wait until I'd answered one question before she asked the next, but it wasn't her way. She talked about Kyle as though he was an old friend that had moved away, and not someone who didn't see her by choice.

So, Mum, how do you spell denial?

'He's OK.'

She sighed. 'He was such a bubbly little boy and then all of a sudden he got *so earnest*. I suppose all teenage boys are earnest, aren't they?'

I didn't think she was looking for an answer, which was a good thing because I disagreed with her – about Kyle, and about boys in general. Most of the boys I knew were about as earnest as a tulle skirt.

'Would you like a coffee?' she asked, and then she frowned a little bit. 'Do you drink coffee?' She blushed. She didn't know.

'I'm right, thanks. I've got a bit of a headache, actually. I wouldn't mind going straight to bed.'

We were sharing a room – two tidy single beds side-by-side with a lamp table in between. Lying down was good but I could still feel the whirling of the rides in my head.

'I'm just going to hop in the shower,' Mum said. 'Don't stay awake for me.'

Mum went into the bathroom, taking her mobile phone. I heard the shower start, but I knew she wasn't in it. She was on the phone to her boyfriend. She didn't come out for ages.

The next day wasn't so bad. We had a big cooked breakfast in the dining room of the guest-house and spent the morning wandering around the shops. Mum bought Kyle a long-sleeved cotton shirt and put it in my bag to give to him.

She should have let me bring Janey after all, because she wanted to ooh ahh at clothes. Lately, Janey had started to talk about clothes all the time. She even wanted to show me shoes in a magazine.

Shoes schmooze.

We stopped at the lolly shop in Leura and Mum let me have whatever I wanted. I shoved some Jaffas in the middle, hoping Mum wouldn't remember that they were Dad's favourite.

When I got home and gave them to him, he smiled and ruffled my hair, but he didn't eat them. He put them in the cupboard behind the latest batch of Janey's mum's almond slice. I wondered if he didn't want them because he knew Mum had paid for them.

Dad made me a big salad. He always made me something super-healthy after I had spent a weekend with Mum. I think he knew how much junk she fed me, but he never said anything. Neither of my parents ever said anything about the other. It was the politest, most silent divorce in the world.

'You look tired, kiddo,' he said, collecting the plates from the table. 'Want to watch a movie with me?'

'Maybe we could read for a while?' I suggested.

'Done,' he said. 'You can pick if you like.'

I grinned. Heading into the lounge room, I yelled over my shoulder, 'Kyle!'

He didn't reply.

'KYLE!'

Dad tut-tutted from the kitchen. 'There's no need to shout. You simply get up, and go to Kyle's door and say, "excuse me, brother, I would like your attention for a moment."'

'WHAT?' came an answering yell from Kyle's room.

Dad shook his head. 'I live in a house full of lions.' He held his hands out and raked the air, as though he had claws. 'Roar, roar.'

I grinned at Dad, and then I tilted my head back and took a deep breath. 'DAD'S GOING TO READ SOMETHING!'

I picked a Stephen King book, *Hearts in Atlantis,* and brought it over to the lounge, where Dad was already sitting down. Kyle sauntered in and sprawled across the armchair.

'Not that one. I've already seen the movie.'

'The book's better,' Dad assured him.

'But I know what they sound like already. It will be all wrong.'

'Let me read you a bit that's not in the movie. Give me ten minutes, and if you're not enjoying it we'll pick something else – deal?'

'Deal.'

Dad always read to us. He reckoned he read to me when I was in a cradle, and I believe him. As we got older we didn't grow out of it. The books just got fatter.

I loved it. At first we were in the lounge-room and Dad was reading words and doing voices, but slowly and without me even noticing it – slowly, just like drifting off to sleep – we'd be somewhere else, and somebody else – watching a scene unfold.

Before I went to bed I unpacked my stuff and gave

Kyle his shirt. He threw it into the cardboard box that he kept in the corner. Since Mum had left he'd taken three full boxes of clothes and presents, and dumped them in one of the charity bins outside the supermarket. They must love it when he does that. I've never told Mum, though. She'd probably hiss at *me*, even though I had nothing to do with it.

Eight

It was going to be a VBD, but it didn't start that way. In fact, it started really well. I finally got a seat on the bench with the others at lunch – the spot on the end. Janey and Hannah had moved one bench over so they could pash their boyfriends.

A girl called Cara sat opposite me. All the others were leaning over a magazine. They spent the whole time talking about celebrity haircuts, make-up and . . .

'Shoes,' I mumbled.

'Yeah. Whacky-doo,' Cara replied.

'Want to play noughts and crosses?' I asked.

Cara shrugged. 'S'pose.'

Cara was pretty good at it, too – much better than Janey. Janey was always crosses, and she always started in the top right-hand corner. Cara changed from noughts to crosses all the time, and every now and then she would turn the page around and look at it from a different angle, which threw me right off my game.

I actually had to think when I played with Cara.

Janey still sat next to me in class. Hannah sat on the

other side of her and she spent most of the lessons facing the other way. I tried to get her attention by telling some jokes. Nothing from Janey, so I pinched her on the back of the arm and stuck my pen in her ear, and then she got really cross and told me I was immature.

We had sport in the afternoon. I sat on the bus by myself, reading James's book. When we arrived at the yoga hall we all spread out across the floor. I sat at the edge near the front.

To my surprise I quite enjoyed yoga. It was very relaxing – too relaxing. The Very Bad Thing happened just as I was moving out of the Lotus Posture and into the Side Bow. All my muscles felt stretched and relaxed.

I had my leg in the air; released the stretch, and – oops! Released something else too.

It wasn't a little silent fart, or even one of those short raspberries that you can cover up by coughing, or pretending it was your clothing scraping on the floor in an unfortunate way – no, this was much worse. It sounded a bit like a whistle.

Whooh.

There was a pause. Then the yoga teacher said, 'Must be the evil spirits.'

The whole class started to laugh. They rolled on their backs with laughter. Why couldn't one of them have accidentally squeezed one out in their amusement? Not one of them did, though – just me.

It was bad.

That night at dinner Dad noticed that I wasn't eating.

'What's wrong with you, kiddo?'

43

'I can't go to school tomorrow,' I said, moving my Pad Thai around the plate. 'I can't ever go there again.'

'What happened?'

There was a long pause while I replayed the incident in my head a few million times.

I looked up at him. 'I farted.'

Dad and Kyle both stared at me for a second. 'So?' said Dad. 'Everybody does it.'

Kyle put down his fork. 'Hey, listen to this one. What's invisible and smells like carrots? A bunny fart!'

'You don't understand,' I said. 'It was ...'

Whooh, whooh, whooh.

'A big fart.'

'What about this one?' interrupted Kyle. 'How can you tell when a clown farts?' He looked at us, grinning. 'It smells funny!'

'Nobody will remember,' Dad said, ignoring him.

'OK, OK,' began Kyle. 'There's this guy, right, and he hasn't had sex before ...'

'Is it you?' I asked.

'Kyle, are you sure that this joke is appropriate?' Dad asked.

He thought for a moment. 'Probably not. Do you want me to tell it anyway?'

Dad shook his head.

'So he meets this girl, right,' Kyle continued.

'Not now, Kyle.'

'And ...'

'No !'

'They ...'

'No, Kyle!' Dad said, slapping his hand on the table-top. Kyle gave up trying to tell the joke, but he had a good long chuckle to himself about how funny it would have been if he had.

'Maybe they will remember tomorrow, but by next week your fart will be all forgotten,' Dad assured me.

He was *so* wrong.

Nine

The next day was very, very bad. It was as awful as the being–naked–in–public dream.

Janey and Hannah were waiting for me, arms folded, barring my way. Cara and the others huddled behind them on the bench.

'We don't think it's a good idea that you Sit With us any more,' said Hannah. 'Everyone is talking about it, Bindy. Everyone.'

'So?' I said feebly.

I looked at Janey, but she wouldn't look back at me. 'Maybe it's best if you sit somewhere else for a little while. Just until it blows over,' she said.

'Fine,' I said, picking up my bag and throwing it across my back. I headed off towards the grassy area near B Block and waited for the bell. I'd always thought it would be the best place to sit, and I was right. The grass was soft and the tall trees let through a dappled sunshine. Janey and the others didn't know what they were missing, perched on their rigid wooden bench.

Still, no sunshine or soft light was going to make my life less hellish.

Anybody who didn't know about The Fart at the beginning of the day sure knew about it by the end. And if they wanted to know who did it they could easily find me by the chorus of raspberries that surrounded me like a big spiny halo.

The raspberries weren't the worst, though. The very worst ones — the ones that made me wish I would spontaneously combust, or maybe astrally project to another dimension for a while — were the boys who whistled, and had somehow managed to mimic the exact same pitch and duration.

Whooh.

I'd never sat on my own in the playground before. Everywhere I looked I saw smirking faces, people whispering to each other, or whistling. I stopped looking around and stared intently at my shoes. I untied and tied my shoelaces for a while, trying to look as though I was busy, but then I thought I might be mistaken for one of the Special Ed kids, as well as a Whistle Farter, so I got out my science book and ruled margins instead.

I'd brought Hannah's clothes in a bag. She hadn't given me a chance to give them to her in the playground, and when I took them to her in class, she backed away from me as though I had a bad case of Mexican flesh-eating worms. After I went back to my seat, she pinched her nose, lifted the bag up with the very tips of her fingers and dropped it next to her backpack.

Janey wouldn't even look at me. I overheard one of

the others say, 'I don't know why you were *ever* friends with her,' to which she replied, 'I know. She's just so bleagh.'

That was the moment. It was officially TWDOML – The Worst Day of My Life.

I had to excuse myself from class, go to the girls' toilets and have a cry. I stayed in one of the cubicles at the end until the bell rang and waited for my eyes to stop being red.

At recess and lunch I took my place by B Block, read James's book and tried to ignore the comments that people made as they walked past me.

It didn't last just one day. It went on the next day, and the day after that, and the day after that. It felt like forever. The next sports day, I didn't go to yoga. I pretended I was queasy and went to sickbay instead. The lady at the front desk pretended to believe me, and because it was the only kindness I'd seen for so long, it made me cry some more.

I finished *The Magician,* and in the following Science lesson, I dropped it on James's desk and kept walking. I thought he might make some smart-alec remark, but he didn't. He didn't pick the book up by the tips of his fingers, either – he shoved it in the plastic shopping bag with the rest of his belongings and then got on with his work.

At lunchtime he wandered over to where I was sitting and squatted down.

'Hi there, Windy Bindy,' he said.

'Go away,' I said, without looking up.

'I've brought you another book.'

'Really?' I asked, lifting my head.

'*Silverthorn*. Have you read it?'

I shook my head. This time I really hadn't.

He sat down next to me. 'Well, it's not quite as good as *The Magician*. I've got the whole series. Do you want to read it?'

'Thanks, James.'

'No problem, buddy – now I know you're a book returner.'

I turned the book over to read the blurb.

James rolled back onto his bum, crossed his legs, and sat there with his elbows hooked around his knees. 'So, what's been happening?' he asked.

'You *know* what's been happening,' I replied.

'Oh, that,' he said. 'Why didn't you put your hand up?'

'What do you mean?'

'You know, like you do in the surf when you're drowning. I could have rescued you.'

Oh yes, of course. Sitting in the middle of the playground, by myself, waving my arm in the air. That would restore my social status. Why didn't I think of it?

I shrugged. 'It didn't cross my mind.'

'I know how important it is to you that we have stuff in common,' he began. Then his face scrunched up in fierce concentration. He dropped his head down to his chest. I could see his cheeks going red. He looked sick, as if he was about to have a hearty.

'James? Are you OK?'

49

After a moment he shifted onto one cheek, lifted up his thigh and let out a short sharp pwarp.

'Phewy!' He waved his hand in front of his nose and grinned. 'There you go. Now we have something else in common. Can we kiss now?'

★ ★ ★

Janey hadn't come over to my place since The Whistle Fart.

'Where *is* Janey these days?' Kyle asked me after school, stealing a piece of my cheese on toast.

'She doesn't like me any more,' I said.

He grunted and then disappeared into his room. After a little while he opened the door and shouted out, 'Bindy!'

He hadn't called me that for ages – it was always Spotty, or Spot-face, or Snotty, or Snot-face.

'What?' I yelled back.

'Do you want to come and play *Battlefield*?'

'Nah,' I shouted.

He wandered out to where I was sitting. 'What about an adventure? It's just point and click, but I think you might like it. The graphics are all 3D-rendered. It's just like a movie, except you're in it.'

I tried to remember the last time Kyle had offered to spend time with me. It had to be about three years.

'OK,' I said.

'Do you want to make us some popcorn?'

I smiled. That was something we used to do in the

old days – make mountains of popcorn and watch Disney movies. Kyle didn't like them so much, but he watched them because he knew I did.

We played for ages and it was good fun working out the different puzzles and clues. After a while Kyle said, 'Janey hasn't stopped coming here because of you.'

'Yes she has. She's got new friends now,' I grumbled. 'She thinks I'm bleagh.'

'I reckon it might be more to do with me.'

'What do you mean?' I asked.

Kyle stared at the screen. The bright lights made shadows on his face.

'The day that we went to the LAN – the day you went to Adele's – we had an argument.'

'What sort of argument?' I asked.

Kyle looked down at the keyboard. 'She was, kind of, going to be my girlfriend.'

I sat back in my chair.

'I know she was your friend, but you didn't seem to be spending much time together any more and she was always hanging around me and laughing at all my jokes. We got along really well. And she put her hand on my arm, or my shoulder, or brushed against me all the time. She said we shouldn't tell anyone, because of you, and so I didn't, but the day of the LAN, when she got in there with all those guys . . . Hardly any chicks ever go there. She was all dressed up and she looked nice, so she was getting a lot of attention. She loved it. She was parading around and swinging her hips and sitting on guys' laps and stuff. So I told her that she couldn't be my girlfriend if she was going to act like such a . . . slut.'

'Did you kiss her?' I asked, even though I didn't want to know the answer.

Kyle nodded. 'Not after that but I did before.'

I shoved my chair away from the desk – not just because he'd stolen my best friend, but also because he'd known her since she was a little kid. He wasn't supposed to feel that way about her.

'I know. What I did sucked,' he said. 'And the worst thing is that she wasn't worth it, not for either of us, because we're family and now we have this *thing* between us – a wrong thing – and she doesn't even care about how either of us feels.'

Kyle stared at me intently. 'Tell me honestly, Bindy, were you the Milk Pig?'

'No.'

'Neither was I, I swear it. So it *must* have been Janey. It's in her nature. She's the Milk Pig – she always will be.'

I always suspected that it was Janey – not because I didn't think Kyle was capable of it, but because he wouldn't have hidden it. He would have woken us up running around our tents shouting, 'Ha, ha! Now you have no milk!'

My stomach felt knotted up.

'The best thing we can do is to *beat* her.'

'We're not in one of your stupid war games now, Kyle,' I snapped.

He shook his head. 'No, I mean, not to let her wreck things for us, because you're going to be my little sister for the rest of our lives and she's just passing through. A couple of years from now we'll be saying, "Janey who?"'

That made me feel like crying. I could feel my throat tighten. I didn't want to say, 'Janey who?' It wasn't that I had planned it or anything, but I'd assumed that we would be best friends, or at least good friends forever. Right now it looked as though I was going to end up by myself, spending my whole dumb life tying and untying my shoelaces for something to do.

Ten

Mum came to pick me up early on Saturday morning.

'What would you like to do this weekend, chicken?' she asked me with a big smile as I got into the car.

'Whatever you want to do, Mum. I don't mind.'

'I thought we might go up the coast. There's a lovely little resort by a lake. I've booked a cabin. It's self-contained, so we'll have to stop and pick up a few things along the way. Maybe you could write a list while I drive? I think there's a notepad in the glovebox.'

I don't know what I was expecting to see in the glovebox — a notepad, obviously, and maybe a street directory. What I didn't expect to see was a pair of gloves, and yet, there they were — men's gloves — spilling over the top, as soon as I unfastened the latch.

'Oh, my golf gloves. Just throw them in the back.'

I wondered how long she was going to keep lying. After all, I'd actually *seen* the boyfriend during the Cinema Incident.

'I didn't know you played golf,' I said.

'Yes, for a little while now. It's great exercise. All that

fresh air. I might try and get a game in at this resort – if there's time.'

I was willing to bet a billion trillion dollars that there wouldn't be. I threw the gloves over my shoulder and leaned forward again, searching for the notepad.

'Let's see,' she began, 'bread, milk, butter, eggs. Do you think they will have tea and coffee? I suppose they will. And something for dinner tonight. What would you like?'

'Maybe we could order in some Chinese?' I suggested.

'Or a pizza – how about that? Let's get some chocolate too.' She gave me a little cutesy smile.

We stopped at a shopping centre before the freeway to get our supplies. Mum bought me a couple of CDs for the trip. The car zipped along and I put my feet up on the dashboard, tapping my toes to the beat.

'How's school?'

'It's OK.'

'Are you getting good marks?'

I shrugged. 'I'm doing all right.'

'That's good.'

Driving, driving. I opened up a packet of chips and offered them to Mum. She took a handful and put them in her lap.

'Doesn't Grandma live somewhere up here?' I asked. We used to drive up to see Grandma when we were small. Kyle and I would fight in the back seat until Mum threatened to drop us out on the road and leave us there. We never dared to call her bluff.

One time Kyle brought his friend Sean. Just as we were going over the Mooney Mooney Bridge, Sean started singing a song. 'I know a song that'll get on your nerves, get on your nerves, get on your nerves. I know a song that'll . . .' And that's as far as he got before Mum stopped the car and put him out.

She actually drove to the next exit before she turned back, and when we picked Sean up a few minutes later, he was crying so hard that we had to take him all the way home. Kyle didn't bring any friends after that.

'Grandma lives up here somewhere, doesn't she?' I repeated.

'She used to.'

'Has she moved?'

Nothing.

'Where did she move to?'

She picked up some chips and stuffed them in her mouth.

'Mum? Where does Grandma live now?'

'Your grandmother is dead.'

I whipped around to face her. 'What do you mean *dead*?'

Mum flicked a glance at me and then shifted in her seat.

'Are you trying to tell me that Grandma *died*, and you didn't tell me?'

'It was all very sudden. It wasn't as though she was sick or anything. She had a stroke.'

'Why didn't *you tell* me?'

Mum didn't say anything.

'Was there a funeral?' I asked.

'Of course there was a funeral!'

'How come we didn't go?'

'It was a school day.'

'I'm sure we could take a day off to go to our grandmother's *funeral*.'

Mum looked in her side mirror – concentrating on overtaking. 'OK. Maybe I made a mistake, but it's done now.'

I leaned forward and switched off the music.

'Mum. She's *dead*!'

Her face contorted just a little bit. She was right on the edge of a hissy fit.

'It's not as if you were close,' she said. 'You haven't asked about her for ages, so I don't know why you are being so dramatic about it.'

I shook my head. 'You see me every second weekend and you don't think to tell me that Grandma *died*?'

She stared at the road. I could see her blink behind her sunglasses. Her lips were drawing tighter.

'Don't you think that you and I should *talk* occasionally, Mum? I don't mean all that flitting-along-the-surface "How's school" stuff, I mean, *really* talk. Like, this boyfriend of yours – how long have you been together now? Three years? Four? And I don't even know his *name*. Don't you think it's stupid – all this "Let's go on a little holiday" thing that you do? Why do we even bother? What about the *movies*, Mum? Are we going to pretend that it just didn't happen?'

Mum slammed on the brakes. I put my hand on the

roof, bracing myself. The car swerved left, right and left again and stopped sharply on the shoulder of the road. My head hit the back of the seat with a thump.

She turned to me and hissed. 'You were *not* close to your grandmother. You only met her a few times, and you didn't see her at all after your father and I separated. This is the first time you've *ever* asked about her. I didn't see any point in taking you out of school, dragging you to a funeral and getting you all upset over someone that you didn't even know. Point two – no, I *don't* tell you about personal things that are happening in my life, but I don't wipe your bottom when you go to the toilet any more, either. There comes a time when you grow up and you start behaving like an adult. And when you're an adult you are entitled to a little privacy.'

I could see little spots of pink on her cheeks.

'Now you listen here, young lady. I try very hard to do something nice for you every single time I see you. I take you to nice places, I buy you nice things, but just lately I've had nothing but disrespect from you. I don't have to put up with it, and I won't. Do you hear me? I can quite easily turn this car around and take you back to your father's – don't you think that I won't.'

Silence. Mum was breathing heavily and her nostrils flared out. A truck swept passed us, and the whole car rocked gently from side to side.

'Then take me back, because I don't want to go with you anyway!' I shouted.

She stomped on the accelerator and we raced along the highway. At the next exit she turned the car around and started heading back the other way. I looked over at the speedometer.

'Mum, you're going way over the limit. Are you going to try and kill me now?'

'If I hear another word out of you, I'll put you out on the road and you can walk,' she said through gritted teeth. She didn't slow down.

I folded my arms and looked out the window. After about ten minutes I leaned forward and turned the music back on.

Mum took the Pacific Highway like a rally-car driver, weaving in and out of the traffic, and bursting forward from the lights. When she pulled up at the front of our place, I got out of the car and slammed the door behind me, not even turning around to see her go, but I heard her. She must have been really angry, because she dropped a big patch of rubber on the road.

I'd always wondered what Kyle and Dad got up to when I was gone. They always seemed to have watched the best movies, eaten the nicest meals and told each other the funniest jokes.

I hadn't been home on a second weekend for years and years, and I couldn't have picked a better one if I'd tried.

Eleven

'What are you doing back, kiddo?' Dad asked as I stormed up the hallway. He was in the kitchen, wiping up dishes.

'Grandma's dead,' I said, tossing my bag on the ground and throwing myself into his arms.

'Oh, Bindy,' he said, patting my head. 'What happened?'

'She had a stroke. She's been dead for ages and Mum never told us.'

'What's going on?' Kyle yelled from his room.

'You'd better come out here, son,' Dad called over his shoulder. He wiped my face with the teatowel. It was damp and smelt of cooking grease and dirty dishwater.

'Yuck!' I said, pushing his hand away.

He held the teatowel to his nose, sniffed, grunted and threw it over his shoulder. Then he lifted up his shirt and wiped my face with the hem.

'Dad!'

'What are you doing here?' Kyle asked as he emerged from his room. He was frowning. 'Are you hurt? Did you and Adele have a blue?'

'Grandma's dead,' I said.

'Oh,' said Kyle. 'She was my favourite octogenarian. What happened to her?'

I explained to them the fight I'd had with Mum in the car. I even told them about how she'd seen me at the movies, but I lied and said that the boyfriend was a woman friend, because I wasn't sure how Dad would take it.

Dad warmed up a serving of lasagne for me and the three of us sat in the lounge-room together.

'What do you remember about your grandmother?' he asked.

'Salmon coloured houndstooth,' I replied. 'And beige Pollyanna shoes.'

'Kyle?' he prompted.

Kyle scratched his head. 'She always smelt kind of dusty – like talcum powder.'

'Your grandmother was a decent woman,' Dad said. 'She was very respectable. She had the most wonderful prize-winning chickens.'

'You're kidding,' said Kyle.

Dad shook his head. 'Nope. She was quite a sought-after chicken breeder. Belgian Barbu Bantams. She used to enter them in the Easter Show. That was when it was over near Centennial Park. We used to go there when you were toddlers to check out Grandma's chooks. Do you remember?'

I shook my head.

'The roosters looked as though they were wearing

tiny feathered waistcoats. Your grandma called them her "little gentlemen". "I must go and tend to my little gentlemen," she used to say. Do you remember what she used to feed us when we went there?'

'No,' Kyle and I said in unison.

'Omelette.'

We laughed.

'Truly! And sponge cake. And pavlova. She must have known about a hundred different recipes for eggs. She kept them all in a big scrapbook in the kitchen by the phone. That's how they did it in those days. They'd go through the women's magazines and take clippings of recipes. That was when women's magazines had recipes, and not just articles on how to achieve the perfect orgasm.'

'Dad!' I protested.

'It's true! They do! You check it out next time we're at the supermarket.' He rubbed his chin. 'Your grandma thought you guys were great.'

After that Dad told us about his parents and about the town where he grew up. It was like the times when he read us a story. I felt as if I was there.

Just as I was pouring myself a glass of water to take to bed, there was a knock at the door. Dad frowned at me. 'Who could that be? It's gone eleven.'

Then we heard the front door open and footsteps coming down the hall.

'Kyle, did you get that?' Dad said.

Kyle stood in the doorway of his room behind us. 'Were you talking to me?'

'Someone's in our house,' Dad whispered. 'Bindy go to your brother. Make sure you lock your door, son. And don't come out until I say so.'

'They wouldn't have knocked if they were robbers,' Kyle said.

'Do as you're told,' Dad said, pointing at him. Dad reached around and grabbed the closest thing behind him – a whisk. Then he snuck across the kitchen and peeked around the corner.

We heard a woman's voice from the hallway. 'You call this supervision?' It was coming closer. Kyle and I poked our heads around the corner so that we could see too.

Marching into the middle of our lounge-room was Janey's mum. Slightly behind her, bent over, mumbling protest and looking faintly green, was Janey.

'What do you call this, John?' Janey's mum yelled, dragging Janey into the kitchen.

'Elizabeth! What are you doing here?' asked Dad.

'She's drunk!'

Then Janey, as if to provide evidence, leaned forward and vomited on the kitchen floor.

Who's bleagh now? I thought, but I didn't say it.

'See?' said Janey's mum.

'Yes. The girl is drunk,' said Dad.

'She was in your care!'

'No, she wasn't.'

'I expected more from you, John. For heaven's sake!'

'Elizabeth,' said Dad quietly, 'Janey hasn't been here.'

'What are you talking about? She's been coming here since she was five years old.'

'Yes, but not recently. The girls had a disagreement. She hasn't been here for weeks.'

'Oh,' she said. She shook Janey's arm. 'You've been lying to me! How long have you been telling me these lies, missy?' Janey' swayed like a broken branch.

'This is probably not the best time to ask her,' suggested Dad. 'Why don't we just pop her into Bindy's room to have a bit of a lie-down, eh?' Then he turned to me. 'Can you make up the trundle, kiddo?'

I nodded and ran down the hallway to my room. After I'd pulled out the bedding, Elizabeth and Dad carried Janey' to the bed and laid her down. She had already passed out.

'Best take her shoes off, but leave the rest. She won't notice,' Dad said. 'Now, how about I put on the kettle?' He gave Elizabeth a smile. I followed them into the kitchen. Dad got some paper towel and spray out of the cupboard and started cleaning up the spew.

'Let me,' said Elizabeth, bending down to help him.

'No, it's all right,' Dad said. 'Bindy, why don't you go to bed?'

'I'm not tired.'

'Read a book then,' he said.

I walked up the hallway and waited, listening.

'I'm so sorry, John. She told me that she was coming here tonight,' Elizabeth said. 'She's been so unmanageable recently.'

'She's a teenager,' he replied.

'Yes, but even so . . . Belinda isn't getting drunk and going out all hours, is she? And those clothes!'

'Go to bed, Bindy,' Dad said.

He had eyes in the back of his head *and* he could see through walls. I took a step backwards.

'When she's home, she's always on the phone,' Janey's mum continued. 'What can they have to talk about? They only just saw each other. I don't think she's eating properly, either. She's always been into the junk food but just recently it's gotten worse. I'm sure she lives on potato chips. I can't remember the last time I saw her eat something green.'

Then they moved to the lounge-room and I couldn't hear what they were saying any more.

Dad and Elizabeth kept talking way after I went to bed. Occasionally they were laughing. I even heard Dad put on some music before I went to sleep.

When I woke, Janey was still in my room and still fast asleep. Her make-up was smeared all over her face and on the pillows as well.

As I made my way to the kitchen I noticed that Dad's door was closed. That was weird because he never closed it. He'd always kept it open at least a few centimetres ever since we were small and would call out to him in the night when we had a bad dream.

I don't know why I opened it. It just seemed wrong for it to be closed – like when you see a knife on the edge of the bench where it could fall on your foot, or a pot on the stove with its handle poking over the side, exactly where you could bump it with your elbow as you go past.

I wasn't *looking* inside. I just saw something odd out

of the corner of my eye, and without even really thinking about it, I looked more closely.

There were two lumps in Dad's bed. There was Dad and then there was another lump, which he had his arm over. Just poking out of the top of the doona I could see a little tuft of brown hair.

My first thought – and I have no idea where this came from – was *When did Dad get a dog?* It was a weird thing to think, but at the time it seemed much more likely that my dad was secretly hiding a very large dog in his room, or perhaps had gone out in the middle of the night to buy one, than that the large lump that he had his arm around was Janey's mother.

Twelve

I closed the door as quietly as I could and tiptoed back to my room.

'Janey,' I whispered, shaking her by the arm.

She murmured and waved her arm at me. 'Sleeping.'

'Janey, wake up!' I shook her harder and gave each of her cheeks a slight slap.

'What is it?' she said irritably. Her eyes were all puffy and her breath was really rank.

'You won't believe it!'

'What?'

'Your mum – she's in there with my dad,' I said.

She sat up suddenly. 'In where?'

'In his room.'

Janey got to her feet, staggering a bit as the trundle bed slid sideways, and marched down the hallway.

'You can't go in there,' I protested.

Janey threw the door open and it hit the wall with a bang.

'Mother!'

Janey's mum's eyes opened and she lifted her head

slightly. We could see that her shoulders were bare.

'Put some clothes on!' Janey ordered.

'Janey, what's going on?' said Elizabeth's sleepy voice.

'Blimey!' said Dad, pulling the covers up around both of them. His eyes were swollen with sleep and his hair stood on end.

'Get out of there and put your clothes on!' Janey said, standing in the doorway with her hands on her hips.

I tried to grab her by the arm and pull her out the door, but she shook me off.

'Janey,' said Dad. 'Why don't you go and put the kettle on? Your mother and I will be out in a minute.'

Your mother and I — I hadn't heard *that* for a long time.

'I'm not leaving until you get out of that bed!' Janey shouted.

Dad propped himself up on his elbows. 'You can stand there and yell as much as you like, Janey, but we're not getting up until you leave the room.'

Janey stared at them for a moment and then she swept out the door, slamming it behind her. She stood in the kitchen with her arms folded, tapping her foot. I put the kettle on and pulled some cups out of the cupboard.

I might have been mistaken but I was pretty sure that I heard giggling from Dad's room. Janey must have heard it too, because she said loudly, 'For heaven's sake!'

A few moments later they emerged. Elizabeth was wearing Dad's dressing-gown and yawning. Her hair was sticking up on top and squooshed at the sides. It looked like a mohawk. Dad didn't look much better.

'What's going on here?' Janey demanded.

Dad put up his hand. 'Coffee first, talk later.'

He got the milk out of the fridge and poured it into a little jug.

Elizabeth sat down at the dining table. 'Janey, this wasn't a planned thing,' she explained. 'I was very distressed last night – you and I will certainly be having a long talk about that later – and John was very understanding.'

'So you *slept* with him?'

Elizabeth tried to smooth down her hair, but it bounced straight back up again. 'John and I are two consenting adults.'

'So this is the message you are sending to us kids, is it?'

Elizabeth sighed. 'Darling, John and I have known each other for many, many years. Ever since Adele left, we've done lots of things together. We went to all your tap concerts, all of your school achievement nights, had parties for both of your birthdays. He's looked after you most afternoons for the last ten years. He's a very good friend to me.'

Janey sat down next to her mother. 'Mum, you can't be with him,' she said urgently.

'Why not?'

'*Look* at him?'

'Janey, don't be so rude!' Elizabeth said.

Janey looked as though she had been slapped.

'How can you do this to me?'

Dad sat down at the table next to Elizabeth and held

her hand. It was *so* weird.

'Janey prepare yourself for a shock.' He leaned forward. 'This is not about *you*.'

Thirteen

Back in my room, Janey was getting ready to go home. She helped me put away the trundle bed.

'We have to break them up,' she said.

'Why?' I asked. 'We don't even know if they are together, really.'

'Are you suggesting that my mother would have a one-night stand?' Janey asked, putting her hands on her hips.

I'd never thought about Janey's mum doing It. Of course, she must have at some stage, because Janey existed, but *now*? Janey's mum wore cardigans with a hanky tucked in the sleeve. Janey's mum was the woman you talked to if you wanted a reliable locksmith, or recipe for Melting Moments, but *rumpy-pumpy*?

I sat down on the edge of the bed. 'I don't see what's so wrong with it. They get along. It's not like they're strangers.'

Janey narrowed her eyes. 'Don't you don't understand anything? When adults Go Out, it's not like when we do it.

Before too long they'll want to move in together, and where will they live? Your dad won't want to move, because he's got the workshop. What if they get married? We'll be sisters.'

I shrugged. 'We were kind of like sisters anyway,' I said. 'Well, we used to be.'

'They might even have other babies,' she added. 'And your dad's not going to let me have friends around.'

Then it occurred to me. She would want to have that horrible Hannah here – HHH. They would help themselves to food in *my* kitchen, and lie around on *my* lounge. And Mitchell too. They would want to slobber on each other on the trundle bed in the middle of *my* floor.

Where would I go when I was sick of them? There would be nowhere to hide.

What about when I had to go and see Mum? I could imagine Janey being in *my* room when I was away – going through all my stuff, moving things around, throwing things away, filling my room with all her junk.

And Dad had rules, but Janey's mum was even stricter. She made a fuss about the weeniest little things. *Use a coaster. Take your elbows off the table. No snacks after eight o'clock – you'll give yourself nightmares. Get those muddy shoes off my clean carpet.* Imagine living with that *all* the time!

Janey saw the expression on my face. '*Now* do you get it?'

After they had gone, I sat down at the table with Dad. He was reading the paper.

'What's going to happen now?'

'I'm going read the paper, and then have a shower. After that I was going to read the paper some more – unless there's something else you'd like to do today. We could go to the beach and get some fish and chips for lunch. We haven't done that for a while.'

'That's not what I meant.'

'What did you mean?' he asked, peering over the top of the paper.

I ran my hands across the tabletop, tracing patterns with my fingers. 'With you and Elizabeth.'

'I don't know' He rustled the paper as he turned the page.

'Are you guys Going Out?'

'We haven't made any plans at this stage, but I might ask her to accompany me somewhere.'

'Dad!'

He looked up. 'What do you want me to say? I don't know what's going to happen next. Do you?'

'Janey reckons her mum will want to get married and have more babies.'

'Is that so?' he said.

I didn't really think they would have more babies, but I wanted him to rule it out. I wanted him to say that the whole thing was a big misunderstanding, because if they really did do It – even if it never happened again – then everything had changed forever. They could never go back to the occasional chat over almond slice and coffee. Janey reckons you won't want to move out because of the workshop, so we'll all have to live here together and she'll have to share my room. And Elizabeth will be the cleanliness nazi, running around after everybody and making us take our shoes off.'

'Indeed?' he said. Then he went back to reading his paper.

I waited for a while but he seemed to be absorbed in the story he was reading. 'So?'

'So what?' he asked, not looking up.

'Are you going to marry her?'

Dad laid the paper flat on the table and leaned on it with his elbows. 'Bindy, I haven't done this Going Out for a while now, so I think it might be a little bit early to tell.'

'But what happens if you do? Will they move in? Do I have to share my room with Janey? What about when she wants to have friends over? I don't like her friends. Are we going to have to use coasters all the time?'

Dad rubbed his eyes and sighed.

'I know this is confusing for you; it's confusing for me too. I don't know what is going to happen – truly. Life doesn't work like that and I wouldn't want it to. Just know that you and Kyle are the most important people in my life, and you always will be. Now, can we just let it lie? Please? I promise to keep you informed.'

Then he flicked the paper up again like a wall between us.

Fourteen

I sat next to James in Science and English. He was good to sit next to because he did his work and didn't try to cover his page up with his arm the way Janey did, in fact he encouraged me. He said I could copy if I would kiss him, and when he caught me peeking at his work he puckered up his lips.

'You know, James, that's not how it works. If I kiss you, it should be because I want to, not because I owe you.'

He shook his head. 'All relationships are about exchange. Both people should get something out of it, otherwise why would you bother?'

'I can't believe you think that!' I retorted. 'Relationships should be about liking someone for who they are – not what you can get out of it.'

He rattled his pen between his teeth before he responded. 'I think it's a pretty sweet deal. You get As in Science and I get to, you know.' He grinned and waggled his eyebrows up and down.

'James!' I wrinkled up my nose.

Then he did something I wasn't expecting. He

grabbed me around the waist in a big, rough hug. I could feel the bare skin of his arms pressing against the skin of mine.

I could smell him, and feel his breath on the back of my neck, and it sent a delicious flicker of static snaking up my spine. At the same time, I was scared – not a normal scared, but something instant and automatic that made me want to kick and fight with all the strength I had.

My stool wobbled dangerously, I squealed, and then he let go. He probably only had hold of me for less than a second, but it was a big second for us.

I looked at him and his eyes were really wide. 'What was that?' I demanded.

He shook his head and stammered, 'I don't know I just had an urge to . . . squeeze you.'

'Well, *don't*,' I said, and slapped him on the shoulder.

★ ★ ★

In Studies in Society I was concentrating on my work when Janey loomed over my desk. 'I'm coming over,' she announced – just like that – and then she turned on her heel and went back to Hannah.

That afternoon Janey gave Dad a dark look as she slid into the back seat of the car.

'What news from the enemy?' he whispered.

'Don't you think we're a bit old for that now?' asked Janey.

'One is never too old to play, Janey,' he replied.

'And is that what you were doing with my *mother*?'

I could see the muscle in Dad's jaw flex. 'You'll use a

civil tongue when you speak to me, Jane Madden,' he said.

Janey caught his eye in the rear-vision mirror and she flicked her head defiantly, but she didn't answer back. Nobody spoke a word until we got home.

Janey wouldn't even let us make a snack. We went straight into my room. Janey got a notepad and a pen out of her bag and sat cross-legged on my floor. I sat opposite her with my back against the edge of the bed.

'We need to make a plan,' she said. On the top of the notepad she wrote *Breaking Up Mum and John,* and then she put a line under it.

'You can't just write a *list,*' I said. 'What if they find it?'

'I'll write it in code. Instead of *Breaking Up Mum and John* I'll put *E minus J.*'

'You don't reckon they'll figure that out?'

Janey chewed the top of the pen. 'We'll burn it after.'

'Why write it down if you're going to burn it?'

She shrugged.

I sighed. 'Why don't you write a better code, like *Ways to break up with Mitchell* and then if they see it they will think it's about you,' I suggested.

Janey nodded. 'OK.' She tore off the page and started again.

'So what are we going to do?' I asked.

'Well, you know how I was with your dad this afternoon? I was showing him that I disapprove. You could do that too. We can let them know how against it we are.'

'Why will they listen to us?'

'Because they have a responsibility to make us happy,' said Janey. 'It was their choice to bring us into the world. They can't just abandon us now that we've become inconvenient to their love life.'

I pondered that for a moment. 'My mum has,' I said.

'Yeah, but your mum's a bitch.'

'Janey!'

She tossed her head. 'Well, she is, isn't she? She's horrible to you – she always has been. You want me to lie?'

'You can't just say stuff like that to people. You've got to have some consideration for other people's feelings.'

'Who am I hurting? She can't hear me. Besides you agree with me. I know you do. You've been whingeing about her for years. *I don't want to go this weekend. Why can't you come too?*'

'That's not the point. It's up to me to say, not you. I don't say mean stuff about your mum.'

'What's to say?' she asked, shrugging. 'My mum is nice.'

I turned around and lay on my stomach. I spoke quietly in case I was overheard. 'Do you reckon they really did It?'

'Nah,' she said, flicking the pen against her knee.

'But they didn't have any clothes on,' I said.

'How do you know? They had the covers pulled up mostly.'

'They wouldn't get out of bed, though. They would have if they had clothes on.' I flicked my eyes towards the hallway.

'Maybe they were in their undies?' Janey whispered, leaning forward.

'What do you reckon they were doing, then?' I asked.

Janey shrugged. 'They were probably just kissing and cuddling.'

I wrinkled up my nose, 'Eewww.'

'Not as eewww as them doing It.'

I covered my mouth with my hand. Then Janey started to laugh. I laughed too.

Dad poked his head around the door. 'What's so funny?' he asked.

Janey gasped, turned the notepad upside down and sat on it.

'Janey wanted to know if . . .' I began.

'Shhh!' Janey said and put her hand over my mouth. I brushed it away.

'She wanted to know . . .'

'Bindy! Shut *up*,' she protested.

Dad shook his head and walked away.

'So what are we going to do?' I whispered, so Dad wouldn't overhear. 'Why would you break up with Mitchell?'

Janey thought about it for a moment. 'If he was doing the sly. If he lied to me. If he got really ugly.'

'Really? You would drop him for being ugly?'

'Yeah!'

'I don't think we can make any of those things happen,' I said. 'We can't make them cheat and we can't make them lie.'

'And your dad's already ugly,' she said.

79

'Is not,' I said.

'Whatever. We'll just have to go back to showing them that we disapprove,' she said. 'Let's give them the Silent Treatment and see how they like it.'

I figured the best way to give my dad the silent treatment was to keep out of his way, so when Janey left I stayed in my room reading until dinner.

After a while I put the book down and lay on the bed with my hands behind my head. I had a poster on the wall at the foot of my bed. It was of a gnome lying on a little hill asleep. There were leaves shading him from the sunlight that filtered through the trees above him. He looked peaceful, and the whole scene had a kind of dreamlike quality to it.

I loved that poster. Mum redecorated my bedroom for my eighth birthday, when I was going through a big fairy phase. I used to stare at that picture and pretend that I lived in Fairyland. I could imagine tiptoeing around that hillside; pushing aside the giant leaves with my magic fairy powers. That picture was the only present Mum had bought me that wasn't functional. I think she bought it because the green of the shading leaves was exactly the same colour as my curtains. She also bought me the complete hardback *Anne* series from *Anne of Green Gables* to *Rilla of Ingleside* because their spines were that particular shade of green as well. They were lined up on a single shelf above my bed and not locked away in the desk drawers like my other books with uncoordinated spines.

Everything that had been put in here since Mum left

was a jumble. Dad liked making things out of car bodies, and so I had a headlight lamp, my wardrobe door was actually an old bonnet and there was a bull-bar on the wall next to the door where Dad hung my shirts after he'd ironed them. It wasn't a pretty room, but it was still my space.

Luckily for me, Kyle had had a particularly successful afternoon on *Battlefield,* and during dinner he gave us a blow-by-blow description of the battle, followed by a detailed lecture on combat technique.

'So, if you manage to *capture* the spawn point, they have nowhere to spawn   their scores come down like a Kasey Chambers song, and the allies win automatically.'

Dad turned towards me. He was about to ask me a question, I could tell.

'But how do you get to their spawn point without being killed?' I asked quickly, as though I was truly intrigued.

'Good question,' said Kyle. 'There are a number of ways.' And then he outlined them in full. He was still telling me about it after we'd all finished eating and Dad had cleared our plates away.

'Do you want me to show you?' he asked.

I couldn't imagine I'd be really interested, but it would keep me out of Dad's way.

'Yes please,' I said and followed Kyle to his room.

It took about half an hour for Kyle to become so engrossed in the game that he forgot I was there. When I snuck out to get my book, he didn't even notice.

At about eleven Dad poked his head around the door

to say goodnight. I gave him a wave and a smile.

'Sleep tight, man,' Kyle said.

This was a pattern that I could live with until the Silent Treatment was over. As long as I stuck with Kyle, he could do the talking for both of us. If I kept a pleasant look on my face, Dad might never even know that it happened.

Fifteen

The next day was sports day and as Dad drove me to school he decided to give me a little pep talk.

'I know that you've been down. So you farted – it's no big deal. Everybody does it. It's nothing to get upset about.'

I stared out the window.

'What you got to remember is that farting is perfectly natural. You would die if you didn't do it – truly!'

I didn't think you would *die*.

'You know what I think?' he went on. 'I think that most kids fart at some stage during the day – it's just that they do little quiet ones, or move to some place where there is a strong draught.'

He paused. 'In fact I know they do it. They used to do it at my school. We used to get a bottle of milk at play-lunch. Some of the boys would drink their milk, fart in the empty bottle and put the lid back on.'

I looked at him with a raised eyebrow.

'Not me!' he said. 'And I don't think any of the girls ever did it. But girls' and boys' intestines can't function that differently, can they?'

I shrugged.

'Is that all that's bothering you, Bindy? Is it Janey? You seemed to be getting along so well yesterday. I heard nothing but giggling from that room all afternoon. Have you made up?'

I nodded.

'That's good news, isn't it? She seemed to go off the rails for a little while there, but you're a good girl. You're a positive influence on her.'

I gave him a little smile.

'Do you know something you're not telling me about? Is it about Janey? Is she doing something wrong? It's not drugs, is it?'

I shook my head.

Dad frowned. He kept flicking his eyes towards me and then back to the road. 'What's wrong with you? Have you got a toothache?'

I waved my hand.

'If you want, I can take you to the dentist. I haven't got a big day today. You haven't been for a while. Are you due for wisdom teeth?'

I pointed to my mouth and gave him the big thumbs up. 'What's wrong with your mouth?'

I gave him the A-OK sign with my thumb and index finger. Dad pulled up to a set of traffic lights and turned to face me.

'Bindy, open your mouth. You haven't gone and got one of those revolting tongue studs have you?'

I poked my tongue out. He inspected it. The light

went green and we started moving again.

'What is it? Have you got laryngitis? Tonsillitis? Are you sick?'

Dad pulled up the car outside the school gates. I opened the door and started to get out.

'Hang on a second,' he said, reaching for my arm. 'What's wrong with you?' He waited. 'Bindy?'

I sighed. 'I'm not speaking to you,' I said.

'Oh. Why not?'

'Janey and I decided that we would not speak to you to show you how much we disapprove of you being with Elizabeth.'

'Maybe you guys should wait until Elizabeth and I are actually together?'

'But then it will be too late.'

'OK. I have noted your opposition. Will you talk to me again now?'

I started to climb out of the car. 'I should probably check with Janey first.'

'You do that,' he said. 'Have a good day, kiddo.'

I pointed to him and then held two fingers up. *You too*.

At school I took up my usual position outside B Block and opened my book. Then suddenly there was a shadow towering over me. It was Janey standing there with her hands on her hips. I looked up at her, shading my eyes with my hand.

'Did you break?' she asked.

'Yeah, a little bit. I only told Dad why we were doing it. What about you?'

'No. It was easy, though. Mum wanted to talk about herself all the way home and then she went out to one of her committee meetings. When she came back, I pretended to be asleep.'

'Dad said we should wait until they are actually together.'

'But then it will be too late!' she said.

'That's what I said.'

'It's going to be harder than we thought,' Janey said. 'We'll have to go to Plan B.'

'What's Plan B?"

'I don't know yet,' she said. 'I'll ring you this arvo and we can figure it out.'

She started to walk away.

'Janey,' I called after her.

She turned around. 'What?'

'Now that we're being friends again, can I come back and sit with you?'

Janey bit her lip. 'I'll need to talk to Hannah about it.'

I asked her again just before recess, and then I asked her at lunch. Both times she palmed me. 'I haven't had a chance to talk it through with Hannah yet.'

What was the big deal? Who made Hannah Plummer the Boss of Seating Arrangements, anyway?

After lunch I went to yoga for the first time since The Fart.

Taking a deep breath, I walked right into the middle of the room and sat down cross-legged on the floor. I expected people to move away from me, but they didn't. They sat around me, leaving the same space as they did for everybody else. I had survived. Things had gone back to the way they were before.

Almost.

Apparently, Hannah was *not* happy for me to Sit With them again. According to Janey, I would ruin their reputation.

'What reputation?' I asked, resting the phone on my shoulder while I turned down the television with the remote.

'You know,' Janey said. I could imagine her stretched out on her lounge and coiling a lock of her hair around her finger. She had this funny way of lying where she half hung off the side, because she wasn't allowed to put her feet up.

'Hannah and I wear the right clothes and boys want to Go Out with us. Other girls look up to us. They want to Sit With us.'

'They do not. Like who?'

Janey paused. 'Well, you do. Anyway, what about Mum and John? Are you going to help with Plan B, or are you going to back out?' she asked.

'There's no Plan B to back out from,' I argued. 'Why don't you call me when you have a Plan B and I'll back out of it then?'

'Well, I hope for your sake . . .' Janey paused. 'Hang on a minute, will you?'

She put her hand over the mouthpiece and then a few seconds later she was back.

'It was just Mum. She's gone down the street.' Then she continued where she'd left off. 'I hope for your sake that they really aren't together.'

'Why don't we just wait and see?'

As it turned out, we didn't have to wait very long – not very long at all. Dad poked his head around the door. He must have just come out of the shower because his hair was plastered down flat. 'I'm going out. I'll be back in half an hour or so.'

'Okies,' I said.

I waited until he was gone. 'That was my dad. He's going out too.'

'*What?*'

'It could be a coincidence.'

'No way it's a coincidence! Battle stations!' she said.

'What are you talking about? We don't have any battle stations.'

'Well, you'd better put your thinking cap on, Bindy, or by next week we could be having this conversation top and tailed in your bed. I know! We should go on strike.'

I curled my lip. 'Strike from what? What could you stop doing that your mum would notice? I don't do anything. Dad does it all. We should just try talking to them.'

'What about a hunger strike?'

'All right, let's make hunger strike Plan C. Plan B is talking, OK?'

Janey sighed. 'Fine, but it won't work.'

I sat on the lounge and waited for Dad to come home. When he came through the door, his eyes were bright and his cheeks were flushed.

'Where have you been?'

He scratched his head. 'I went to have coffee with Elizabeth.'

'Did you just?' I said.

'Bindy, we know you girls don't approve. That's partly what we talked about.' Dad sat on the lounge next to me. 'We don't have any plans to get married and move in together. But we have a lot in common – you two girls, for example. We agreed that it would be very nice to have someone to go the movies with, or maybe the theatre. We could go out for dinner occasionally – that sort of thing.'

'You can take me and Kyle out for dinner.'

Dad smiled. 'Yes, but it's not quite the same thing.'

'So what you're saying is that you're going to have a casual affair with this woman?' I asked, crossing my arms.

Dad went into the kitchen. He called over his shoulder. 'Don't you have homework to do?'

'Maybe,' I replied sullenly. 'Are you going to help?'

Dad and I sat at the kitchen table to tackle my algebra. The problem was that between the question and the solution was an hour-long lecture on the history of mathematics, beginning with how cavemen determined the range of their arrows. I kept yawning and tried to hide it by keeping my mouth closed. After the fourth or fifth stifled yawn, Dad asked me if I needed to go to the toilet.

'No, why?'

'You look uncomfortable. I thought you might need to liberate some surplus.'

'Dad!'

When he moved on to logic and philosophy I told him I didn't need his help any more and flipped to the answers in the back of the book instead.

He stood up and began to make the dinner.

'I don't know why you need Elizabeth anyway,' I said. 'You've got heaps of friends. You've got the guys in the workshop.'

'Yes, but I'm the boss. Elizabeth is someone I can talk to. Someone I can have fun with.'

I snorted.

Dad put his hands up. There was a little furrow of annoyance on his brow that I hadn't seen before. 'This is how it is going to be from now on, Bindy. You're going to have to get used to it.'

Janey was right. Plan B sucked.

Sixteen

The next day at lunch, I walked up to where Janey was sitting with Hannah and Mitchell watching the basketball game.

'We're going to have to go to Plan C,' I said.

She didn't answer.

'Janey?'

'Sorry, were you talking to me?' she asked, shading her eyes with her hand.

'Yes, I was talking to you. That's why I said "Janey". If I was talking to somebody else I would have used *their* name. Plan C – the hunger strike. Remember?'

She looked over my shoulder at the boys playing basketball.

'I can see that you're busy right now with your *new* friends,' I said.

Janey exchanged a glance with Hannah, and Hannah said, 'I think it might be time to talk with her, don't you?'

Janey sighed and stood up. 'Come on then.'

We started walking around the edge of the court.

'If Hannah won't let me sit with her, why don't you come and sit with me? Like we used to,' I started.

Janey opened her mouth and then shut it again.

'What's the problem? It's not about the fart thing. Nobody even mentions that any more.'

This was the part where Janey was supposed to say, *Yeah, you're right — it's dumb, isn't it? Come and sit with us. Hannah will just have to get over herself.* Or even better, *Hannah is getting boring anyway. I'll come and sit with you.* But she didn't. Instead she said, 'I think we've just grown apart.'

I stopped walking. 'What?'

'OK.' She put her hands on her hips and exhaled. 'I've been trying really hard not to hurt your feelings, Bindy, but I don't like doing the stuff that you want to do. I haven't for ages. I don't want to watch cartoons and make up elf dances. I think it's boring and dumb. I've grown up and . . . well, you haven't, Bindy. Hannah likes the same stuff that I do. We have boyfriends and we go out at night. We watch MTV and E.'

I felt my face go red.

Janey continued, 'I don't want you to be upset or offended. I just wish you'd make some of your own friends. Maybe you could hang around with someone who's more . . . on your level.'

★ ★ ★

I had no idea where I was headed. I could hardly see through the blur of angry tears. They hadn't spilled over yet, but it was close. I was marching across the play-ground, with my hands clenched into fists, and then an idea crossed my mind. I decided to visit Kyle in the Senior Common Room.

'Junior alert! Junior alert!' said one of the boys, sitting near the door.

Kyle looked up and saw me. 'Hello, Spotty. What do you want?'

'Can you come here for a minute?' I whispered.

He came to the door. He knew it was something big. We had an unspoken rule about not associating at school.

'Janey said . . .' I started. My lip was trembling. I tried to hold it in, but I was really struggling. 'Janey said . . .' and then I burst into tears.

'Oh, Bindy. Come here,' he said, and he put his arms around me. I never ever thought he would do that – especially not in front of so many people. It made me cry harder.

'Look, Kyle's getting it on with one of the juniors,' said one of the boys.

'That's his sister, stupid,' replied another.

'Isn't that sweet?' one of the girls said.

Kyle held me at arm's length and his eyes searched my face. 'What did Janey say?'

'She said she didn't like me any more. She said I was boring and immature, and I needed to find someone more on my level.'

Kyle nodded. 'That's what she said to me too. She's really not worth it, Bindy, truly.' He sounded just like Dad.

'But I don't have anyone to sit with,' I whispered. 'I don't want to go back out there.'

Because I'm afraid that I will cry and she will see, and then that really would make me sad and immature and the last thing I want right now is to prove her right.

I didn't have to say it out aloud. Kyle knew it already. He frowned. 'I'd let you sit in here with me, but I've got soccer training now.'

'I thought you gave it up,' I said.

Kyle smiled. 'Not playing – coaching. I don't mention it at home because Dad would want to get involved – really involved. You know how he gets.'

'Maybe I could come and watch?' I asked.

'OK,' he said.

We walked along the corridor, stopping at the sports room to get the equipment.

'How are they going?' asked Mr Moody, the PE teacher, as he opened the storeroom.

'I reckon they'll make the Regionals,' Kyle replied.

Mr Moody nodded. 'Nice. We haven't had a decent junior team since . . .' He paused. 'I don't think we've *ever* had one.'

He bent down to move some equipment aside, and kicked the balls out to Kyle. 'We haven't got jerseys that'll fit them. We can put them in the bigger ones, I suppose.'

'They've been working really hard, sir. It would be good if they could wear jerseys that fit.'

Mr Moody frowned. 'You'll have to ask the parents for the money. My budget's stretched as it is.'

'The parents have already bought boots and uniforms for their clubs. Maybe we could raise the funds ourselves?'

Mr Moody shook his head. 'It's a good idea, Kyle, but I just don't have the time to organise it.'

Kyle nodded. He tucked a soccer ball under each arm and walked towards the field with me in tow.

A rabble of Year 7s stood at the edge of the field. Some of them had changed into sports gear already. One boy stripped off his school shirt to reveal a brand-new, bright green surf shirt underneath.

'Michael, Michael, Michael,' said Kyle. He leaned forward with his hands on his thighs so that he was eye level with the boy. 'Are you a surfer?'

Michael shook his head.

'I didn't think so. What you've got there is a fine example of an Aunty Shirt. Do you know what that is?'

Michael shook his head.

'Anyone?'

All the boys looked at each other and shook their heads.

'Then gather round, because I'm going to tell you something important.' Kyle got them all in a huddle.

'An Aunty Shirt is mostly a recognisable surf brand like this one.' Kyle tapped the logo on the boy's chest. 'It's called an Aunty Shirt because aunts usually buy them for their nephews with the best of intentions. But you'll find that the surfers can get a bit-aggro when they see these brands being worn by people who aren't surfers. They can tell because it's not worn out and bleached by the sun. Do you understand?'

The boys nodded.

'Don't feel bad about it, Michael, because you weren't to know. It's a nice shirt, so you can wear it at training, but I don't want you walking around the corridors in it, OK? I can't have my star offensive player all bruised and battered. If you want to wear it, make sure it goes through the wash a couple of times and has a good long stint on the line in full sun. You might want to tear it a bit too. Otherwise, just stick to the sports uniform. You can't get yourself into any trouble that way. All right?'

'OK,' said Michael.

Kyle stood up again. 'Right, let's start with some stretches.'

He took the boys through a warm-up routine and then they jogged back and forth across the field for a while, dribbling the balls to each other. After that he sat them cross-legged in a circle and went through some strategy.

Just before the bell he sent them to the change rooms – making sure Michael covered his shirt before he left.

'You should be a teacher when you grow up,' I said as we walked back across the field to the school buildings.

Kyle shrugged. 'They're good kids. I like them. It's a shame we can't dress them. It would make them feel good – as though the school was proud of them. They don't cost that much.'

'Why don't *we* hold a fund-raiser?' I asked.

Kyle frowned. 'I should be spending more time studying as it is. It would be good for them, though.'

For the whole rest of the day I wrote down ideas for fund-raising. It was better than tying and untying my shoelaces.

Seventeen

When I got home the phone rang. It was Mum.

'Hello?'

'His name is Phillip. He's thirty-eight. He's an accountant,' she said. 'What else do you want to know?'

Thirty-eight didn't make him that much younger than she was. I took the phone down the hall and into my room, shutting the door behind me. I didn't want Dad to overhear this conversation.

'Does he have kids?' I asked, keeping my voice low.

'No.'

'Has he been married before?' I sat down on my bed.

'No. He was engaged once, but it didn't work out.'

'Why not?'

'I don't know,' she replied gruffly.

'Did *Phillip* go to Grandma's funeral?' I asked, pulling one of the pillows onto my lap.

'Yes, he did. He was there to support *me*, and besides, he met her several times.'

'You never took us to see her, but you took Phillip?' I asked.

'Your grandmother was very happy to see me with Phillip. He's an educated, elegant man and your grandmother approved of him very much.'

'Meaning?'

'Meaning what?' she asked.

I flicked my eyes towards the door. 'Meaning that Dad is not educated or elegant,' I whispered.

'Your father and grandma never got along – not from the very beginning. I *dreaded* going to see her with John.'

I was about to say, *He told me he liked her*, but then I thought about it. Dad never said he liked her. He just said she had funky chickens and that she liked us.

'Does Phillip know about me and Kyle?'

'Yes.'

'Does he want to meet us?'

She paused for a second. 'I'm sure he would love to meet you.'

'But has he *said* he would like to meet us?'

'He's very busy. He plays sport on the weekend – golf, squash, triathlons.'

'He doesn't want to meet us, does he, Mum?'

She took a deep breath. 'Parenting is not one of Phillip's key priorities at the moment.'

'And is parenting one of your *key priorities*, Mum?' I knew even as the words were coming out that I had stepped over the line.

'Don't be ridiculous,' she hissed. 'You listen here. I rang to *share* with you because you asked me to. I didn't have to. You're going to have to get used to the idea that just because you ask a question doesn't necessarily mean that you're going to get the answer that you want to hear.'

Silence.

'I think we've talked enough for now, don't you?' she said.

'Yes,' I whispered.

'I'll see you at the weekend,' she said, and she hung up.

I lay back on my bed and hugged my pillow. So, the man who had stolen my mother had a name. He was Phillip. He played sport and had 'key priorities'. I didn't like him already, but I still wanted to meet him so that I could find even more reasons to dislike him. More, I wanted him to want to meet me, and when he did I would be indifferent and . . . adolescent. Then one of his 'key priorities' might be leaving.

But what was all that stuff about Grandma?

I went in search of Dad. He was on the lounge, reading. 'You never said that you hated Grandma,' I said.

'I didn't hate her,' he replied, looking up. 'We didn't always see eye-to-eye. Anyway, she's dead. I didn't see any point in holding a grudge. Besides, I'm sure that wherever she is, she's less engrossed with earthly concerns than she once was.'

'What do you mean by that?'

He put the book down and patted the seat next to him. I sat down.

'Your grandmother was very big on social hierarchy. She thought I was a gold-digger,' he said with a wink.

'She wanted your mother to marry someone who wore a tie to work and had a membership at a country club.' He smiled. 'I don't think they have a dress code in the afterlife. Wouldn't they all be in something loose and free-flowing?'

I had a mental picture of my grandmother – who was so fastidious – sitting in a white wicker chair in heaven wearing a long salmon-coloured kaftan with a ghostly chicken on her lap, and it made me laugh.

Eighteen

When Dad came in from the workshop the next night, I knew something was up. He had his shower, the same as always, but instead of pulling on a pair of daggy trackies and a T shirt, the way he usually did, he put on a pair of pants and a short-sleeved, collared shirt. He even ironed it. And he was wearing shoes. He never wore shoes in the house – he just padded around on his long, flat, hairy feet. Apart from that he looked different, somehow, I couldn't put my finger on it.

Then he started peeling prawns. That was really unusual, because it was a Wednesday. We only ever had prawns on a Monday, or maybe a Sunday if it was winter, because our garbage was collected on Tuesday mornings and if you left the stinky seafood scraps in the bin it stunk up the whole laneway next to the house and wafted in through Kyle's bedroom window. You'd think there was an elephant carcass in his bed the way he went on about it.

'Do you know where the whisk is?' he asked.

It was on the hall table. He'd left it there after the

Drunken Janey Incident. I went to fetch it for him. 'Thanks, kiddo,' he said, 'I've been looking for that for days.'

'So what's happening?'

'Can you pass me the saffron?' he asked.

I handed it to him and he grabbed a whole tea-spoonful and shoved it in the pan. That was really, *really* unusual, because saffron costs more than gold, and he only ever used the tiniest pinch.

'Who's coming over?' I asked.

He took a spoon and ladled out some of the mixture. He cupped his hand under it and held it in front of me. 'Try this. Does it need salt?'

I tasted it. 'It's OK.'

'Just OK?'

'It's good.'

'Not too spicy?'

'*Dad!* Who-is-coming-over?'

'Didn't I tell you?' he said innocently. 'Liz said she might drop by later on.'

Not Elizabeth – Liz.

'This is a whole lot of work for someone who might drop by,' I commented.

Dad grabbed me by the shoulders. 'Tell me honestly, how do I look?'

I stared at him. 'Your left eye's a bit red.'

'Yes, I know, I accidentally stuck chilli in it. Stings like a bugger, I can tell you. It'll go away, though. I had a haircut,' he said, patting down his hair at the sides. 'What do you think – generally?'

He'd had a haircut — that's what it was. I looked at him closely. Generally, he looked better than he had for ages. He was still wrinkly, but they were all happy, smiling wrinkles. His eyes were sparkly and he had rosy cheeks. He looked hopeful.

'You look good.'

'What about this shirt?' he asked, plucking at it. 'I've had it for so long that I thought it might have come back in fashion again.'

'Dad, you look fine.'

He looked up at the clock on the microwave. 'Half an hour,' he said. 'She said she might be here at about eight. Can you put some music on?'

I wandered over to the CD player. 'What do you want?'

'What about Barry White?' he called out over the sizzle of the wok.

'Make-out music!' I protested.

'Too obvious? What about Bryan Ferry?'

'That's sooo ancient! What about this Latin jazz stuff that you have?'

'Done,' he replied.

There was a knock at the door. Dad thrust his head around the corner and gaped at me — panic-stricken. 'I'm not ready,' he whispered. He had a brief struggle with the apron he was wearing, and when he finally got it over his head, his hair was sticking out at the sides the way it always did.

'You'll be fine,' I said.

I pushed the CD player closed, pressed Play and then went to open the door.

Janey was leaning against the front wall with one foot propped against the bricks. She had her arms folded. Elizabeth was standing behind her. She was wearing long dangly earrings and clutching a bottle of wine in a brown paper bag.

'Hello, Bindy,' said Elizabeth smiling brightly – too brightly.

'We're not staying,' said Janey. 'They can't make me stay.'

'Janey, go inside,' said her mother. She was still smiling at me but her voice had a tremor of frustration in it. I guessed that they had been arguing in the car.

'You can't make me,' she replied.

Elizabeth sighed. 'Spend the whole night on the front step. I don't care.'

Janey pushed herself off the wall with her foot and sat down on the step with her back to us.

I stood aside. Elizabeth handed me the bottle and walked past me into the hall.

Dad met her in the lounge room and gave her a quick peck on the lips. Elizabeth gave out a little surprised, 'Oooh', and then laughed nervously. They both started talking at once.

'I've made . . .'

'I brought a . . .'

They both laughed.

'After you,' said Dad.

'No, you first,' said Elizabeth.

'Please, I insist,' said Dad.

I sighed. 'Dad's made Choo Chee,' I said, 'and Elizabeth brought a . . .' I pulled the wine out of the bag. 'A red.'

'Sounds delish,' said Elizabeth.

'Lovely,' said Dad. 'Let me open that for you.'

He took the bottle of wine from me and went into the kitchen to get the bottle-opener.

'Is Janey with you tonight?' he asked.

'Janey is choosing to wait out the front,' Elizabeth replied.

'Well, I'm sure if we leave her out there on her own she'll come in sooner or later. It's not like Janey to miss out on some attention. Bindy, can you please set the table?' he asked. 'With the tulips.'

'Are you sure?' I asked.

The tulip linen was for best. It had belonged to his mother and she had hand-embroidered yellow tulips and blue cornflowers around its scalloped edges. It was so special that, as far as I could remember, we had never used it. Every couple of years, during the spring-clean, Dad brought it out, washed it, ironed it and put it away again. Liz must be super special.

'What if you get Choo Chee on it?'

'There's no point in having something beautiful if you're not going to enjoy it,' he replied.

After I had set the table, I hung around in the kitchen for a while, listening to Dad and Elizabeth talk. Elizabeth poured the glasses of wine and then she took two coasters from the windowsill and put the glasses on them. Coasters on the kitchen bench? You don't need coasters on the kitchen bench! I flicked my eyes towards them and nodded to Dad. *See? See?* But he seemed to be ignoring me.

'Why don't you go and see what Janey's doing?' he suggested.

Oh yes, that would be great! Maybe she could call me some more names?

'Off you go,' he said, gently hitting me on the backside with the teatowel.

Kyle came out of his room. 'How are you, Elizabeth?' he asked, reaching across the benchtop to pluck a stalk of coriander from the cutting board. Then he leaned against the counter, munching away.

'Call me Liz, please, after all we're . . .' she gave her head a funny little shake and her earrings jangled ' . . . closer now.'

Kyle didn't say anything for a moment. He just chewed away on his sprig of coriander with his mouth open. That was another pet hate of hers. I wondered if she was going to pull him up on it now that she and he were . . . closer?

'Sure. Liz it is then. Cool.'

Dad had his back to Kyle and from the corner of my eye I saw him roll his eyes at Elizabeth ever so slightly. What was *that* all about? Whose side was he on?

Nineteen

Janey wasn't out the front. I skipped down the steps and peered over the fence, looking along the street, but I couldn't see her. I peeked down the narrow passageway at the side of the house. She was leaning against the wall, next to the bin, holding a cigarette between her thumb and forefinger.

'What are you doing?' I asked.

She jerked around with a little gasp. Then she put her hand on her chest. 'Bindy, you scared me.'

'Are you *smoking*?'

Janey shook her head. 'Not tobacco.' Her voice was strained as she held the smoke in her lungs. She let it out, and it wafted away in curlicues above her head.

'Is it marijuana?' I couldn't believe it.

She held it out to me. 'Want some?'

'No! Janey, it's drugs!'

She shook her head. 'It's not bad for you. In fact, it's good for you. Research shows that it has heaps of medical uses. It can even cure cancer. But the big pharmaceutical companies don't want to let the public know. They don't want people growing their own cures in their back yards. The companies have the government in their pockets because they pay for its campaigns.'

'Who told you all this?' I asked.

'Mitchell's brother Nick,' she replied, and took another drag.

'Is he the same guy that's selling it to you?'

She shook her head and let the smoke out. 'He doesn't make me pay. He reckons he spills more on the carpet than I smoke, so it doesn't matter.'

'He doesn't make you pay *yet*,' I said. 'He'll wait until you're hooked and then he'll make you pay for it.'

'It's not addictive,' she replied, 'That's just propaganda. Some people are just more prone to addiction than others – it's like asthma.'

'Nick told you this too, did he?'

Janey nodded. 'So do you want some?'

'No thanks.'

'How do you know you won't like it?' she asked.

I flicked my hair out of my eyes. 'I don't want to become a druggo.'

Janey snorted at me. 'One drag hardly makes you a *druggo*. You should try it before you make all these assumptions that it's so bad. If you don't like it, at least you'll know what you're missing out on.'

'I'm not going to, Janey,' I said. I edged past her and headed for the back door.

'Your loss,' she said, stubbing it out and following me. From the kitchen I could hear Elizabeth laughing, then

Dad joined her with his deep chuckle. They were really yakking it up.

Janey walked in and flopped down on my bed. I sat down on the floor with my back to the wall and stared at her. Her eyes were red and glazy.

'Kids, dinner's on the table,' Dad called down the hallway.

I began to get up.

'What about Plan C? The hunger strike?' Janey asked me. 'I knew you'd back out.'

'You just don't want them to see you on drugs.'

She narrowed her eyes. 'You're *encouraging* them.'

'Am not.'

Janey crossed one leg over the other and looked around the room. 'Which end do you want? I think I'll paint my half of the room purple – or maybe orange,' she said.

'That's it. I'm going to tell,' I said, standing up.

She nodded towards my gnome poster. 'That will definitely have to go.'

'You can't. It's special to me.'

Janey shrugged. 'We all have to make sacrifices.'

We stared at each other.

'Do you think being a druggo is *mature*?' I asked.

She sat up suddenly. 'Maybe I'll just wait until you're at your mum's and I'll pull it down and tear it into little tiny pieces.'

'It's laminated.'

'Well, I'll use scissors then!'

I shook my head. 'You truly are a horrible person. I don't know why I ever liked you.'

Janey looked out the window 'Well, you'd better get used to it.'

We had to break Dad and Liz up as soon as possible. I didn't care about them, but I knew that for me, living with Janey — the new, mature Janey — would be hell.

Twenty

The weirdest thing happened in Computer Skills. I was sitting by myself, as per usual, when Cara – the one who played noughts and crosses with me – sat down and started talking.

'Have you finished that English assignment?' she asked. 'I haven't done it yet – I don't really know what to do. There's a history assignment due the day before, isn't there? I like history better . . .' *blah, blah*.

It was all very suspicious. I gave her the information that she wanted about the assignments, and I expected her to get up and walk away, but she didn't. She just sat there yakking it up.

'What are you doing on the weekend? I was supposed to go ice-skating, but I'm not now I think I might just have a quiet one – maybe watch some movies . . .' *blah, blah*.

At the end of class, instead of saying, 'Well, that was fun', and going back to Hannah and the others, she stood waiting for me to pack my things and then followed me down to B Block. When she got to my spot, she dropped her bag and sat cross-legged.

'What did you say you were doing this weekend?' she asked.

I decided to keep being friendly until I figured out what this was about.

'Well, actually I'm supposed to go somewhere with my mother,' I said. 'I'm a bit nervous, because last time I saw her we had a fight.'

'Doesn't she live with you?'

'No, my parents aren't together any more.'

'That must be sad for you,' she said. 'I couldn't imagine it.'

I blinked. 'I'm not sad at all. I don't know how they ever got together in the first place. They must have got along at the beginning, before I was born, but they are complete opposites. I couldn't imagine them being together now.'

Cara reached into her bag and brought out a packet of biscuits. 'Want some?'

'Thanks. So,' I began. *Why are you Sitting With me?* 'What's happening with you?'

Cara looked at the ground for a minute, nibbling on the biscuit.

'I used to hang out with Hannah. She was my best friend most of the way through primary school. Hannah's dad is some kind of businessman and they go overseas all the time. In Year 3, Hannah went to live in Kuala Lumpur. She came back for Year 4 and then in Year 5, they went to Jakarta. I wrote to her twice a week. She came back for Year 6, and then in Year 7, the other girls came and sat with us.' Cara paused for a moment. 'I'm a little bit pissed off, because I put in a lot of effort to be her friend, even when she was away. I could have just found other friends. And now it's as though she's forgotten everything.'

I knew how that felt.

'Hannah's always been bossy – telling me what to do and what to wear – but now she's with Janey, it's all gone super-powered. Do you know what I mean?'

'Yep.'

'They look down their noses at everybody – even their own friends. They think they're better than everybody else. It's hard work trying to stay on their good side all the time.'

I nodded and took another biscuit.

'And now they're getting so *mean*. They encourage each other. You're different. You don't seem to let what people say bother you and that's kind of how I'd like to be. Is that OK?'

I frowned, puzzled. 'Is what OK?'

'Can I sit here?' She continued, 'I thought it would be good for you too, because you're here on your own, mostly – when James isn't here.'

I smiled. 'Sure.'

She looked relieved.

Cara sat next to me in Maths and Studies in Society. It was weird sitting with someone again – very distracting. In Science I sat down in my normal spot next to James. Cara pulled up a stool and sat on the other side of me. James frowned and cocked his head towards her.

'Is it OK?' I whispered.

James nodded, but he didn't look convinced. He wrote in the back of his book and pushed it towards me, covering it slightly with his arm so Cara couldn't see. It said, SPY?

'I don't think so,' I murmured.

Cara leaned on the desk, resting her head on her hand. 'So are you guys Going Out or what?'

'We haven't, like, had sex or anything,' he replied.

I gave him a *shut-up* punch under the desk. 'We're just good mates,' I replied.

James underlined the word in his book three times.

'I'll be careful,' I muttered to him.

★ ★ ★

Liz and Janey came over that night. Janey and I sat on opposite ends of the lounge watching telly while Dad and Liz cooked dinner.

'So now you're all pally with Cara,' she said.

I held my hands up like horse blinkers.

'See? This is exactly what I'm talking about,' she said.

I started saying, 'La, la, la,' over and over, until she stopped talking.

After a moment, Janey began again. 'She's a complete loser, you know. I suppose she came crying to you. What did she say about us? I bet she said, "They *don't care about my feelings*". Sooo sorry for herself. She's a great big compliment leech. You'll get sick of her pretty soon.'

'So is the hunger strike over yet?' I asked, changing

the subject. The smells coming from the kitchen were very inviting.

She shook her head. '*I'm* not eating.'

'I saw you eating today at school!' I said.

Janey crossed her arms. 'It's like the forty-hour famine. We only have to do it when they're watching.'

'It's a dumb idea,' I said. 'Especially if you're not even going to do it properly.'

'You don't get to make the rules. It was my idea. You didn't have any ideas, remember?'

We both shut up then, because Liz came into the room. I had my feet up on the coffee table and she looked at them and frowned. I almost took them down, but then I remembered that this was my house and I was allowed. 'Dinner will be ready soon,' she said.

'We're not having any,' said Janey sullenly, and then she leaned back, put her feet on the arm of the chair and drummed them up and down.

Liz put her hand over her eyes. 'I'm not seeing you do that, Jane Madden. I'm not seeing it.' Then she walked back into the kitchen.

'Are you going to your mum's this weekend?' Janey asked me.

'Why?'

'No reason,' she said. But there *was* a reason, I found out later.

'I'm going to my room to do my homework,' I said, standing up.

'Hang on a second, you didn't tell me what she said.'
'Who?'

'Your new buddy Cara-the-Loser, of course.'

'Cara's not a loser. She's nice – a lot nicer than you. You're just rude,' I said.

'I've always been this rude,' she replied.

Twenty-one

Mum picked me up on Friday afternoon, and didn't drop me back until Sunday afternoon, so I missed the whole incident. If I'd been there, I might have saved myself a whole lot of trauma.

I hopped into the car and waited for Mum to say, 'What do you want to do this weekend, chicken?' But she didn't. She just said, 'I feel like something all-you-can-eat.'

We drove for a while and stopped at a family restaurant near the beach. It was full of kids' birthday parties and big extended families all chowing down. The waiter gave us two empty plates. We lined up at the bain-maries, filled our plates, and then slid into a booth next to the window. 'How's school?' she asked.

'Pretty good.'

'Are you getting good marks?'

'Yep. Great marks.'

She stared at me for a moment. 'I ask you that because I'm interested. I want you to do well at school, Bindy. A good education is very important. You're a smart girl. You always have been. Very stable. You can be anything you want to be.'

'I know, Mum.'

'What do you want to do?' she asked. I shrugged.

'How's little Janey Madden?'

I looked down and moved my food around the plate. 'Janey and I don't really get along any more.' I peeked at her quickly and then looked away. 'Dad and Elizabeth are kind of . . .' I trailed off.

Mum was either pretending, or she hadn't heard me. 'You two were peas in a pod when you were little,' she said. 'So who's your best friend now?'

'I don't really have one.'

'You're in a group now? That's how it happens. My best friend at primary school was Francine Aldemar. She went to some Catholic school and I never saw her again. How about that? I wonder what happened to Francine?'

I took a mouthful. 'How's Kyle?' she asked.

'He's all right.'

'What's he been doing?'

I sipped my drink, trying to buy some time. She always asked about him, and it wasn't fair that I had to find endless ways of avoiding her questions all the time.

'He's coaching the soccer team at school.'

Mum smiled. 'That's great! I thought he'd given up on soccer after his accident. I'm so glad. I told him at the time that he should get straight back on that horse, but he got so huffy about it that I'd thought it best to leave it. And now he's done it on his own. I'm so pleased to hear it.'

Her little speech sparked my curiosity. Neither of them had ever really said what their beef was about.

'So, tell me about this soccer team,' she said, slipping out of the booth to get herself another helping.

I slithered out behind her. 'Kyle wants them to have new jerseys, but the school won't buy them. They don't have enough money.'

'You can get the money somewhere else,' she said.

'Oh yeah, like where? People don't just give out money,' I replied.

'Yes they do. It's called sponsorship,' she said, grabbing a big chunk of garlic bread. 'That's what the professional teams do. How much do they need?'

I shrugged.

'You could always run a raffle, or have a car boot sale,' she said.

When we'd finished, she wiped her mouth with her serviette. 'Do you want to have dessert here? Or shall we pick up some icecream and have it at home?'

'Are we going to your flat?'

Mum nodded.

'Will *Phillip* be there?'

'Phillip's away this weekend.'

'Let's go home,' I said.

Mum's place was one of those split-level, executive-style apartments that are all chrome and Perspex. It was probably bigger than our house. It looked different since the last time I'd been there. She had redecorated. There were glass sculptures in display cases, and black-and-white photos on the wall of her and Phillip holding hands on a yacht. They looked as if they were in one of those expensive perfume ads.

Everything matched. It was nothing like home, where everything was odd, multi-coloured and thrown in together, like a curio shop.

'This looks pretty flash,' I said, walking around. 'So clean.'

The room that I used to stay in had been turned into a study. I dropped my bag in the corner next to the door. Everything was black or in shades of teal. There were a few papers on the desk, but it was very tidy – not like Dad's office, with half a dozen overflowing 'in' trays, his car-furniture, and dirty coffee cups all over the place.

Mum followed me into the room, leaning her elbow against the doorframe. 'It's easy to keep the place clean when . . .' she began. She blushed, then she tried to change the subject. 'Do you want a drink? I'll get you a drink.' She disappeared out of the door and into the kitchen.

. . . *when you don't have children.* That's what she was going to say.

I walked back into the lounge room and picked up a tall glass cat. I turned it over in my hands. 'How old were you when you had Kyle?'

'Twenty-four – nearly twenty-five,' she answered. I could hear her opening and closing the kitchen cupboard doors.

'And you were married when you were twenty-two?' She came into the room and put down the can of soft drink she was holding. She took the glass cat from me and returned it to its place on the side table.

'Was that young?' I asked.

Mum tilted her head to the side. 'It was pretty normal in those days. Most of my friends were married or engaged. There were a few who weren't.'

'I mean for you?'

Her eyes narrowed a little bit. 'What are you asking?'

'Just wondering.'

'Let's watch a movie,' she said. She opened the cupboard under the television. It was full of DVDs. 'Why don't you come and pick one?'

I knelt down next to her and flicked through the titles. 'What about Alfred Hitchcock?' I suggested. 'Isn't he supposed to be good? I've never seen any of his movies.'

'Blasphemy!' she said. 'All right, how about *Vertigo*? If you like it we can watch *Rear Window* after. We'll have ourselves a little Hitchcock double feature.'

I shrugged. 'Sounds good to me.'

Mum filled two bowls with icecream. We sat next to each other on the lounge and watched the movie. It was like something I would do with Kyle. As the credits rolled up, she asked, 'So what do you think of Hitchcock?'

I ignored her question. 'Was Kyle a planned baby?' I asked.

She sighed. 'Belinda, what's with all the questions? What is it that you want to know?'

'I just want to know how it used to be. That's normal, isn't it?'

'I don't think that's what you're asking.' She pulled one of the cushions onto her lap, running her fingers around the hem. 'Is it about why I left? Is that what you want to know?'

I folded my arms. 'Did you want us?'

'Of course I wanted you.' She rubbed her eyes. 'I won't deny that it was your father's idea. He knew how to hold you, and what to do to make you stop crying. He seemed to know how to do all those things.'

She stared at me, and it felt accusing. I had to look away.

'Can we watch the other movie now?' she asked.

'I just want to know,' I said.

She frowned. 'What? What do you want to know?'

I shrugged and wiped at a spot of icecream that had melted onto my shirt.

'I know you think I *abandoned* you. You think I should have fought your father for custody. But I have never pretended to be a good mother. The best thing I could do for you was to let you stay with your father.'

I still wouldn't look at her.

'John and I don't get along any more. We grew apart, but he takes good care of you both. I trust him to raise you.'

Because you can't be bothered. I thought it, but I didn't say it.

'*Now* can we watch the other movie?' she asked.

'I'm a bit tired. I might go to bed,' I mumbled.

'What do you want from me?' she hissed.

I hated it when she got angry with me. It made my heart beat really fast.

'OK, so I'm a bad mother. Is that what you want?' she asked.

I felt tears well in my eyes. I covered my face with my hands so that she couldn't see. I didn't want her to say that. I wanted her to say she would try to be a better mother; that it was important to her; that she *missed* me and wished I was around. I wanted her to say that it broke her heart every time she dropped me off. That's how mothers were *supposed* to feel. They weren't supposed to forget you existed the minute you walked out the door, and be happy that you weren't making their flat untidy.

I didn't want a confession – I wanted . . .

'I want you to love me,' I blurted. The second I said it I felt stupid and pathetic. Tears of frustration ran down my cheeks.

Mum put her arms around me. 'Of *course*, I love you, you nitwit.'

I leaned against her shoulder and she rocked me. 'Belinda, you've got to come to terms with the fact that I'm never going to bake cookies, or join the P & C. It's just not *me*.'

She patted my back. 'I do my best for you, chicken, but it's complicated. I don't think you have any idea how hard it is for me having the whole world know that John can take better care of you than I can.'

Twenty-two

On Sunday morning Mum came into the room just after I had woken up.

'Morning,' I said.

She tapped the doorframe with her manicured fingernails. 'Do you like this room?'

I looked up at the ceiling and let my eyes wander around the walls. There was a sliding glass door leading out to a small terrace. It didn't have the ocean views that Mum's room had, but it had quite a pleasant aspect over the valley. 'Yeah. It's nice.'

'It's just that when I . . . when *we* first moved here I thought that we could make this . . . sort of, your space, but you didn't seem to like it.'

'No, I like it,' I replied. 'I've always liked it, but I never really felt as though it belonged to me, that's all. Every time I came here it was so much yours and . . .' I *didn't want to open any drawers or cupboards because, if I did, I'd see things that I wasn't supposed to know about.*

Mum nodded.

We went out for brunch at a little café at the shopping

centre near Mum's flat. We split the newspaper in two. Mum read the financial pages while I read the funnies. After we'd finished eating, Mum sighed. 'Do you want to do something today?'

I shrugged. I wasn't used to being the one who made those decisions.

'Do you want to go shopping? Do you need anything at the moment – clothes, books, or anything?'

I shook my head.

'Do you want me to drop you home?'

'Yes please.'

While Mum paid the bill I surreptitiously looked at my watch. It had only just gone midday. Our 'quality time' was getting shorter and shorter.

Just as I hopped out of the car, Mum leaned across the seat.

'Can you find out how much Kyle needs for those jerseys? I might be able to come up with some ideas if I know how much we're talking about.'

'OK.'

When I walked in the door, I knew something had happened. Dad was sitting on the lounge, and he looked grim. He didn't even say anything about me being home early.

I dropped my bag on the floor in the hall. 'What is it?'

'Come and sit down, kiddo.'

The look on his face made me think someone had died. I sat down next to him and he held my hand.

'Liz and I went out last night,' he began. 'Janey said she wanted to use Kyle's computer for some history assignment. He was at a friend's place, so we let her stay. We weren't gone for very long – maybe three or four hours.'

He paused.

'Did you have an accident? Is Elizabeth OK?'

Dad held his hand up, shushing me. 'Liz is fine,' he said. 'Janey . . . Janey had a little gathering while we were away.'

'What do you mean?'

'She had a party. Not exactly a party, because there were only four or five of them here, as far as we know.'

I glanced around the room. 'Did she wreck the place? What got broken?'

'Nothing out here. Bindy, she had the party in your room.'

I started to stand up. Dad held onto my hand, making me sit down again.

'We've cleaned up most of the mess. It wasn't too bad. Nothing was broken – there were some bottles and empty chip packets – that sort of thing. There's just one thing.'

'What?'

He cleared his throat. 'Your poster has been . . . defaced. I tried to clean it off, but they've used something permanent.'

When I stood up this time, he let my hand go. I ran down the hallway and into my bedroom. It looked exactly the same as when I had left, except for a small stain in the middle of the carpet. It *looked* the same, but it *felt* different. Somebody had drawn a large penis on my gnome in thick black texta. It was awful. Even if I were ever able to clean it off, I would always see it there in my mind. I would have preferred Janey to cut the poster up the way she had threatened to.

I wanted to punch her.

I turned to see Dad standing in the doorway. He walked over and put his arms around me and I buried my face in his shoulder. 'I know, kiddo. It's a terrible, terrible thing for her to do.'

I thought that was the worst of it. It wasn't. The worst part didn't happen until two days later.

Twenty-three

On Monday Cara was waiting for me at our spot outside B Block. I told her about Janey's party.

'That is soo slack!' she said. 'Your dad ought to have her arrested for breaking and entering.'

I shook my head. 'Dad wouldn't do that. Besides, she was invited.'

'What are you going to do?' she asked.

I shrugged. 'I don't know. At first it was just lots of little things, but now it's like she's a completely different person. The Janey who was my best friend would never do what she's done. I used to wish we were sisters, and now I don't really want to have anything to do with her. But . . .'

Cara stared at me glumly. 'I know. At the same time you just wish some things could be how they used to be.' I nodded.

When I walked in to Studies in Society, Janey was sitting on the other side of the room with Hannah. We ignored each other. Janey was pretending not to look at me, but I could see her glancing over.

Hannah was gesturing to Mitchell, and he shook his head. Something was up. I wasn't sure what it was, but I knew that the three of them had been in my room on Saturday night and it made me so angry. I had a vision of them all sitting there in my space, and I hated them.

I wanted to shout at Janey and let her know exactly how I felt about what she'd done, but instead I told Cara about Kyle's soccer team and how they needed to raise funds for jerseys. I leaned in close to her whispering, smiling and giggling as though it was something really exciting that we were talking about.

'We could do that together,' Cara said. 'It would be fun.' She clapped her hands together and grinned way more enthusiastically than she should have, given what we were talking about, but I knew she was doing it to help me. She had just as much interest in making Hannah and Janey annoyed as I did.

We passed a note back and forth.

Mum said we could hold a raffle.

We can go down the street and ask the shops to donate prizes.

What about the music shop? CDs would be good. Especially signed ones.

And free concert tickets with backstage passes!

Mr Gabler became quite cross with us because he knew we weren't concentrating, but whenever he asked us a question, we were able to answer it. We irritated Janey too. She was watching Cara and me closely.

What about a plant stall?

What we need is a jersey tree.

When I passed that one to Cara she laughed out loud as though it was the funniest thing in the world. She flicked her eyes up at Janey and down again, with a knowing smirk on her lips.

Cara leaned forward and let her hair hang down, hiding her face from Janey and Hannah. She drew a small flower on the page with five petals, and I put my hands up to my mouth in mock surprise and mouthed, 'really?' as if she had just told me something shocking. Cara nodded sagely, and then we both giggled.

Janey glared at me with her eyes narrow and piggy.

At the end of the class, Hannah passed by my desk. 'You missed a great party on Saturday night,' she said.

I tried to think of something smart to say and couldn't, but Cara was faster.

'Nice venue, shame about the people,' she said.

'At least we know how to have a good time,' Hannah retorted.

'Breaking and entering with three druggos, that's what you call a party, is it?' Cara asked.

'There were four,' Hannah said.

'Yeah, nice one,' I said, giving her two thumbs up. Hannah gave us a dirty look and then marched out the door.

Cara and I grinned at each other, and then headed up to the senior common room to talk to Kyle about our fund-raising ideas. As we walked along the corridor Janey marched up behind us.

'Bindy, I want to talk to you,' she said.

I stopped. 'I don't want to hear anything you have to say.'

'She doesn't want to talk to you,' Cara said to her, linking her arm in mine.

'You don't even know what this is about, so just butt out,' Janey said to her. She turned to me. 'Remember what I said? I was trying to show them that they can't just go off and ignore us.'

'Get lost, Janey,' I said.

Janey put her hands on her hips. 'Well, what are you doing to help? Nothing! I have to do *everything*.'

I turned quickly and stood right up in her face. My face was so angry and red that I thought it might explode. She took a step backwards. 'I didn't tell, Janey,' I said through my gritted teeth. 'That was the deal. You said you would wreck it if I told, but I never said *anything*!'

Then I grabbed Cara's arm and started dragging her towards the stairs.

'Told about what?' Cara asked.

'I'm not telling.' I glared over my shoulder at Janey. 'I'm *still* not telling!' I shouted at her.

Cara and I kept walking, leaving Janey standing in the hallway with her hands on her hips and her mouth open. Kyle was already talking to the Deputy, Mr Clemens, about fund-raising ideas. We found him just outside Mr Clemens's office.

'Here come your little supporters now,' Mr Clemens said. 'I was just telling Kyle how impressed I am. Instead of complaining, you've used your initiative to find a solution. I certainly hope that you will consider running for Captain at the end of the year, Kyle. We could use someone like you.'

Kyle blushed. I was proud of him. He would make a great Captain.

'We've done this plenty of times before. There are lots of local businesses that have supported us in the past,' Mr Clemens said. 'Why don't you three stand up on assembly today to announce it?'

Cara went pale. 'I can't do that – not in front of all those people.'

'Of course you can,' replied Mr Clemens.

When it was time for assembly, I led Cara down to the quad and we sat on three seats at the side of the dais with the other announcers and waited. There were all the usual things – permission slips for excursions, keeping the playground clean, results of recent sporting events. Then Mr Clemens asked Kyle up to the microphone.

'This year we have a very promising Under 13s soccer team that we expect will make the Regionals and perhaps the State finals,' said Kyle. 'We haven't had such a strong Junior side before, and we need to get them some jerseys, so that when they go out there and win for our school, nobody will have any doubt where they came from.'

Kyle stood to the side. 'Go on, Bindy,' he said.

Cara clutched my arm. 'I can't go up there. I'm going to wet myself.'

'You are not,' I said, and I pulled her on to the dais. She shrank back – hiding behind Kyle.

I stood there looking out at all those faces. I'd never seen a crowd from this angle before. They rippled and moved like bees on a honeycomb. Then I started to make out individual faces. I felt naked standing there with only the microphone stand to protect me. My heart was beating fast and I could feel adrenalin cold in my stomach. My throat was closing up and I had to squeeze the first words out.

Standing on tiptoes, I reached up towards the microphone. 'To raise funds we're holding a competition.' My voice was very loud, and seemed to come from everywhere. I took a step backwards.

Kyle leaned over and tilted the microphone down for me. The crowd snickered.

My throat felt like it had closed to a pinhole. Looking out I saw Janey's face in the crowd. She was sitting towards the back on the right-hand side, quite still, and staring at me. Her face was blank. I stood there for what felt like about ten minutes.

'You can help this worthy cause,' I said.

Then I saw something else. It was like a Mexican wave going through the crowd, but it spread out like fingers from the back of the quad. Something was being passed from one hand to the other across the crowd. What was it? It looked like rolled-up balls of paper. There was more than one. The crowd wrinkled like waves. I counted. There were four objects being passed around.

'Buy a raffle ticket,' I started again. And then I stopped. The crowd started murmuring as the paper balls were passed from hand to hand. It was getting louder.

'. . . for the chance to win prizes,' I continued.

What *were* they?

The things were halfway across the quad now – two heading across the back, one down the middle and another one being passed quite quickly down the left-hand side. The murmur was getting louder and louder – no individual voices, just a roar.

And then I saw. One boy tossed it into the air and it fanned out and dropped down like a little parachute. It was underwear – a pair of navy-blue cottontails. You can buy them in packs of seven from any supermarket in the country.

Now everyone was shrieking, yelling and laughing.

Then, off to the side, another pair sailed up into the air. These ones were pale blue with pink flowers. I felt all the blood draining from my face. Probably half the girls sitting in the quad were wearing them – or something very similar. But there could be no mistaking whose they were. Dad had made me write my name in neat print letters on the hems of all my clothes before I went to camp last year.

I looked up the back to Janey's face. She wasn't laughing. She was just sitting there, looking straight ahead. My ears were ringing. When I blinked I saw neon spots in front of my eyes.

How could she do this to me?

I felt dizzy, as though I was going to faint. I put my hand up to my mouth and stepped backwards, colliding with Mr Clemens standing behind me. He took me by the shoulders and moved me out of the way.

Breathe.

'That's enough now,' he said into the microphone. 'Staff, please collect . . . those things.'

The teachers quickly picked their way through the crowd, grabbing the undies as they went. Everyone was still yelling and hooting.

Kyle grabbed me by the arm and led me off the dais. 'What's wrong?' he asked.

'They're my undies,' I whispered. Tears of embarrassment welled in my eyes.

Cara put her hands to her face. 'Oh my God. That's my worst nightmare.'

Kyle and Cara stood in front of me, shielding me from the crowd.

'That's enough!' called out Mr Clemens. The crowd began to quieten.

He stood there looking out at the students. 'You might think this is a joke, but it's not funny. This *deplorable* behaviour goes completely against our school spirit, and I'm ashamed of each and every one of you for participating. We will find out who did this, and they will be severely reprimanded.'

He stood there staring out at them. 'This will never, *ever* happen again.'

Silence.

'Dismissed,' he said, waving his hand.

Twenty-four

The School Counsellor, Mrs Sumati, escorted Cara, Kyle and me into the Deputy's office. My undies were in a plastic bag in the middle of the desk. Mr Clemens was on the phone.

'No, they're both quite well.' He gestured for us to sit down. 'But there has been an incident with Belinda . . . No, nothing like that, but we would like you to come down here . . . Great, John, we'll see you soon.'

Mr Clemens hung up the phone and pushed back from the desk. 'Belinda, I'm *deeply* sorry for what just happened out there.'

I burst into tears. He handed me a box of tissues. They all watched me cry and I felt stupid, but I couldn't stop either.

Kyle put his arm around me. 'Bindy, it's OK. I'm going to punch her face in.'

'Who do you think is behind this?' asked Mr Clemens.

'Janey Madden,' replied Kyle. 'She's gone completely

psychotic. She had a party in my sister's room when none of us were there. She invited people into our *house*. She needs slapping.'

Mr Clemens sat back. 'She broke into your house? Perhaps there's a police issue, as well?'

Kyle shook his head. 'It's not as simple as that. Janey's mum is sort of seeing our dad.'

Mr Clemens sighed. 'Well, I can understand how that would complicate things. Still, it's not an excuse.' He stood up and went to the microphone for the PA system.

'Jane Madden to the Deputy's office, please. Jane Madden.'

His voice echoed across the empty quadrangle.

Mrs Sumati leaned towards me. 'This new relation-ship must be difficult for you, Belinda. Especially if you and Jane don't get along.'

'Bindy's fine. Bindy's normal,' said Kyle. 'It's Janey who needs the counselling. She's insane, I'm telling you – not to mention an absolute nymphoid.'

'So, there is some animosity between you and Jane as well?' Mrs Sumati asked.

'Animosity? She's a hag-faced, bitch-breathed, spite-ful little slut-bucket. She needs a good spanking.'

'Thank you, Kyle, we've heard your view,' said Mr Clemens. 'Belinda, do you have any evidence that Jane is responsible?'

'Come on, Bindy. You know it was Janey,' said Kyle. 'Tell them.'

'She must have stolen Bindy's undies when she had that party,' said Cara.

I looked down at my hands. 'Janey said she would wreck my stuff.'

'She made a threat?' asked Mrs Sumati.

I wasn't going to dob her in. I couldn't – not after I'd made such a big deal about it. Besides, what could they do? Give her a lecture – and then what? It would just escalate things. Janey would find a way to get me back, and it was clear that she was willing to go way further than I ever would.

'Belinda, do you understand what bullying is?' asked Mrs Sumati.

'Yeah.' I could see where this was going. She wanted to give it a name so she could look it up in her discipline procedures manual. 'But I'm not some geeky crybaby who can't handle herself in the playground.'

There was a knock at the door. Mr Clemens ignored it. 'I would like all three of you to sit in the foyer and write a statement about what happened today. After you've finished you can go back to class. Belinda, when your father arrives, you can go home if you like – if he says it's OK.'

He handed me the shopping bag and I took it from him, blushing.

'Now I'd like to hear Miss Madden's side of the story,' he said.

'I hope you've got a straitjacket,' muttered Kyle.

Janey was waiting out in the corridor with her arms folded. 'Dobber,' she said.

'I didn't dob. I didn't have to. It was so obvious that it was you,' I said. 'I hope you get detention forever. I hope you get expelled.'

'There's no evidence that I did anything,' she said.

'That's enough, girls,' Mr Clemens said. 'Please come in to my office, Jane.'

'You can't prove it was me.'

'We'll discuss that in a minute.'

Janey stalked into the office and the door closed behind her with a click.

Twenty-five

Dad arrived while Cara, Kyle and I were writing our statements. There was such concern in his eyes that for a moment I got all teary again. He gave my shoulders a squeeze before Mrs Sumati took him into her office to explain what had happened. Cara hugged me before she went back to class.

'I'll ring you after, OK?' she said.

In the car I watched the streets whip past, but in my mind I was replaying the assembly over and over again. All I could see was the undies floating down through the air. Every time I did, I felt hot with embarrassment and my eyes prickled.

When we got home Dad put a big spud in the microwave for me. While we were waiting for it to cook, we sat down at the kitchen table together.

'I don't understand it, Dad. I really don't know what's going on with Janey. When she wanted to sit with Hannah, I didn't fight it. I just went along with it. When she didn't want to hang around with me any more, I was hurt, really hurt, but I didn't say anything. Why does she have to be nasty to me? Why does she keep doing these mean things?'

'You're asking me how women's minds work?' Dad asked. 'I haven't got a clue! I'm a simple man. It's all a great mystery to me.'

I sighed and rested my forehead in my hands.

There was a pen on the table in front of Dad and he picked it up and flipped it from end to end on the placemat.

'You know I don't like to talk to you about your mother because I get the feeling that your relationship is pretty strained as it is without me interfering.'

I nodded.

'But I will tell you one thing.'

I waited for him to continue. He kept flipping the pen faster and faster.

'When she told me she was going to leave, I wasn't surprised. I was sad, but not surprised. Things hadn't been good for a while.' He paused. 'We were sitting here pretty much like you and I are now. You kids were in bed. She told me and I nodded, and we sat here quietly. After a while she packed some of her things and she left.'

I sat very still. Neither of my parents had ever told me anything about their break-up. One day Mum sat down with us in Kyle's room and said that they were going to have a trial separation, but that she would still see us on weekends, and that's how it had been ever since.

'She came around a couple of days later to give me her new number and address, and to sort out a few other things.'

He looked up at me briefly, and then looked back at his pen again.

'We talked. That is, she talked and I listened. She was angry. I could tell, although her voice was quite controlled. When you live with someone for fifteen years you know when they're angry, even when they try to hide it.'

He paused for a moment. 'Just before she walked out the door she turned and said, "You're not even going to try to stop me, are you, John?" I didn't know what to say.

'It hadn't crossed my mind to stop her. I didn't want her to go, but she was free to make her own choices. Then she said that she was right to leave, because I didn't care enough about the marriage to fight for it.'

He lifted his hands palm up. We stared at each other.

'But if she wasn't leaving, you wouldn't have to,' I said.

'Precisely,' he replied.

The phone rang and Dad stood up to answer it, leaning his weight on his knuckles. He looked older when he stood up like that. He tucked the phone under his chin. 'Yep, no problem. See you later, love.'

Dad held the phone out to me, waggling it. I stood up and took it from his hand. 'Bindy?' It was Liz. 'I'm so sorry.'

I didn't know what to say, so I mumbled, 'Doesn't matter.'

'No, it *does* matter. It must have been terrible for you.' I held the phone against my ear and watched Dad cooking. He cut the spud in two, scooped out the contents and broke an egg into each half. He sprinkled them both with cheese and put them under the grill.

Liz went on. 'Janey's not coping very well with all this. I can see why she's been fighting so hard. She knows how close you and Kyle are, and I am close to John. She's worried that she'll always be the odd one out.'

So the solution is to embarrass me in front of the whole school?

'That's no excuse for her behaviour today,' she said, 'but I just thought it might help you understand.' Liz sighed in my ear. 'Sometimes when people are angry and scared, they lash out at the person closest to them.'

'Why?' I asked, frowning.

'Well, I suppose it's because when it's all over, that person will forgive them.'

I grunted.

'Your dad and I really want this to work out, Bindy, but it has to work for everybody, and that's going to take time. This is not about taking sides. It's about finding a way that we can all fit in together, and that means everyone has to compromise a little bit.'

As I hung up the phone I wondered why it always seemed to be me who was doing all the compromising. Dad glanced up at me. 'How did you go?' he asked.

I shrugged. 'Liz thinks I should forgive her. It's all a part of fitting in together.' I snorted. 'Like *that's* ever going to happen.'

Dad leaned down, looking into the grill. 'Maybe you

should think about it? You know Janey never thinks anything through. She just does the first thing that comes into her head. She has no self-discipline.'

'But she does nasty stuff!' I complained.

He turned the potatoes around with the tongs. 'You broke Janey's arm. That must have been very painful. She forgave you.'

I slapped my hands on the table, not believing my ears. 'I didn't *mean* to break her arm. It was an accident!'

Dad shrugged. 'You pulled the step out from under her. Janey's broken arm was a consequence that you could have foreseen, if you'd thought it through.'

'I was *eight*!' I shouted.

He put the spuds on a plate and brought them over to the table, placing them in front of me. Then went back into the kitchen to pick up his keys.

'I have to go out now, kiddo.'

'Where are you going?'

'To pick up Janey from school. She's been sent home. Liz can't get the time off work to fetch her. It's probably best if I drop her at home – I mean *her* home.'

I couldn't believe it. 'But *I'm* the victim here. How can she ask you? You're supposed to stay and look after me. You can't go and get her – no way!' I said.

'Way,' he answered. 'There isn't anybody else who can do it.'

We stared at each other while I tried to think how to stop him.

'What if I have some sort of anxiety attack while you're not here? What if I freak out and bang my head

145

or something? Can't you see how traumatised I am?'

'Have your spud. Spuds are great for anxiety. I'll try not to be too long,' he said. Then he walked out the door.

Not fair! Janey gets a nice caring father who's always there, and what do I get? A neat Nazi who thinks I should be everybody's doormat.

I picked at my potato and wondered what was happening at school. Was everyone laughing about it? Were there any other 'souvenirs'? I abandoned the spud, and went to my room to check, pulling out a pad to make an inventory of all my things.

Janey's stuff was already starting to creep in. Her clothes were all mixed with mine in the basket of clean washing Dad had left on the end of my bed. A few of her schoolbooks were scattered across my desk, along with a magazine, a stick of mascara, a hairbrush and half a packet of chewing gum. A pile of my books had been pushed off the desk and lay in a crumpled heap on the floor next to the waste-paper basket.

I squatted down and flattened out their covers with the heel of my hand, feeling the anger rising in my chest. How did they expect me to fit in a whole other person in this space? There was no room. Even if we got double bunks, there was still the problem of all Janey's junk.

The worst thing was Janey didn't have to go anywhere. She would be here all the time, and I would become the visitor. At first they would call it 'the girls' room', but how long would it be before they started calling it 'Janey's room'? And then what would happen? I could imagine them taking all my stuff to the tip when I wasn't there. I'd come home one Sunday night and find that all I had was a hammock strung up on the front porch. I had a vision of Liz standing at the front door, barring my entry. *We all have to compromise, Bindy.*

My chest felt tight. Janey was squeezing me out of my own life and Dad and Liz were on *her* side. It was so unfair. I gathered up Janey's things and threw them into the hallway. 'This is *my* room!' I shouted.

I'd never thought about running away from home before, but at that moment I just wanted to run down the hall, bash open the front door, and keep running and running away from here. But where would I go?

The phone rang. I marched down the hallway and picked it up. 'What?' I barked.

'Not a good time?' asked Cara.

'Oh, it's you. I'm sorry.'

'It's been a big day, hasn't it?' Cara said.

'You can say that again.'

'It's been a big day, hasn't it?' she said, and we both giggled. It was a relief to talk to Cara. She seemed to be the only person who was on my side.

'So what happened? Is it really bad?' I asked.

'Well,' she said, settling in for a big story. 'After I went back to class, Mitchell, Hannah and Lucas were called to Mr Clemens's office and I didn't see them for the rest of the day. I don't know what happened, but everyone is saying that they've been suspended. Half of the Year 11 girls came down into the quad at lunchtime. They were looking for Janey and Hannah and telling everyone that they were going to hit them. Most people reckon it wouldn't be right for Kyle to do it, because he's a boy, but the Year 11 girls didn't end up punching them anyway, because Hannah and Janey had been sent home by then. The whole school knows that half of Year 11 wants to smack them out. I wouldn't be rushing back to school if I were them.'

She paused for breath. 'All the people I talked to said that it was really slack. Most of the girls say that Janey and Hannah are bitches and nobody wants to sit with them any more. Heaps of the boys came up to me and asked if you were OK. Even Mr Gaoler stopped me in the corridor to find out how you were.'

'That's nice,' I murmured.

'James was so worried about you. There was talk that he was going to fight Mitchell, but most people say that Mitchell wouldn't do it, because all the Year 11s are on James's side. James said he might ring you later.'

I felt a little thrill run up my spine at the thought of it.

'So are you guys Going Out or what?' she asked.

'Why?' I asked.

'Well, he's kind of cute, and I thought maybe if you weren't Going Out with him . . .' she trailed off. 'Of course, I wouldn't do anything if you like him.'

'Does he like you?' I asked.

She paused. 'Well, he's flirty. He told me that he'd had a dream that he'd spanked me, but it wasn't his fault because he can't control what happens in his dreams.

Do you know what I mean? The other boys say stuff that's pretty graphic, but when James says things it's so unsubtle that it's funny. And he's safe. With some guys you look in their eyes and you're not sure that they would stop if you asked them to, but James is so bumbling.'

A prickle of indignation ran right through my limbs, and something else too – disappointment. James had been my friend when others wouldn't. I thought he liked me.

I had been sure that he more than liked me, but now it seemed he just liked any girl.

I didn't want him to be with Cara. Right now they were *my* friends. If they got together, then I would be *their* friend. It was out of the question. A friend of a couple – there was nothing more thirdy than that.

Twenty-six

Later that afternoon the phone rang again. It was Mum.

'I got a message from the school earlier. Tell me what happened? I've been worried,' she said.

When I didn't reply she said, 'Are you still there?'

'If you were so worried, how come you didn't come down and pick me up then?' I asked. 'How come you waited all this time before ringing?'

She exhaled into the phone. 'I don't have the luxury of abandoning my business whenever the fancy takes me. People rely on me. Besides, I knew your father would be able to handle it. And he's closer.'

'Maybe you should delegate all the worrying to him too?' I snapped.

She paused. 'Belinda, are you at home?' she asked.

'Yes.'

'Are you safe?'

'Yes.'

'Well, stop complaining then. If I had come to the school I would have taken you back to work with me. It wouldn't have been convenient for either of us.'

Her logic was so frustrating. 'This is not about where *I am*,' I said, 'this is about the fact that you can't be bothered. Once – just once – it would be nice to know that you were *genuinely* worried.'

'I *was* genuinely worried,' she said.

'You should have been there when I needed you,' I insisted. 'Or at least . . .'

'Hang on, I've got another call,' she said.

'*Mum,*' I yelled, but all I could hear was Hold music. I hung up the phone and flopped on the lounge with my arms folded.

She rang back about a minute later. 'I thought I put you on hold, but I must have lost you.'

'*No,*' I said, 'I hung up on you.'

'Oh,' she replied. 'Is Kyle at home?'

'This is not about Kyle. It's about *me!*' I shouted.

'Yes, and I rang to see if you were OK, and you're obviously fine. By the way, your favourite colour is blue, right?' she asked.

'What's that got to do with anything?'

'Pale blue?'

'*I* don't know. I suppose. Why?'

'Is Kyle there?' she asked, ignoring me. 'I have some good news for him.'

'What?' I snapped.

'I've just donated a thousand dollars towards his soccer jerseys. That should be enough, shouldn't it? That fellow Clemens seemed happy.' She paused. 'Belinda?'

I exploded. 'I can't believe that's what you rang about. *I'm* the one who was in trouble – not Kyle. You always care more about him than me. *Dad* talked about it with me. Dad has handled it the way he always does. You haven't had to do anything. Even Liz . . .'

I stopped abruptly. Oops! That's twice the cat has come scrambling out of the bag and up the curtains. I listened, but she stayed quiet. I could tell she was still there though, I could hear her breathing.

'So it's really none of your business,' I added.

'None of my business?' she repeated.

'That's right,' I said.

'None of my business? You think your dad does everything for you, do you? Everything? Not quite, young lady. Why don't you ask him who pays the bills? Now, if you don't mind, I'm really very busy,' she said. 'You ask him, and then we'll talk.' And then she was gone.

I lay on my bed and fumed. I bet if Kyle had his undies passed around the school she'd be there in a flash.

After a while Dad appeared in the doorway. He stood with his hands on his hips looking down at Janey's things that were puddled around his feet.

'I don't want any of that stuff in my room,' I said, scowling.

His eyebrows raised a little bit. 'Fair enough. Should I throw it all out into the street, do you think?'

'I don't care,' I said, and then I flopped over, turning my face to the wall.

'I'm going to make some toast. Do you want some?' he asked.

I sat up suddenly. 'Who pays the bills?' I demanded.

'I beg your pardon?'

'You heard me,' I said.

He frowned. 'Bindy, I appreciate that you've had a hard day, but I won't accept that tone of voice from you, or from anyone else.'

I slumped down on my elbows, while I tried to decide what to do. I was in the mood for a good long shouting match, but Dad was no good to yell at. He never shouted back. He usually held up his hand and said, 'I'm not a lion. I refuse to enter into debate with anyone who roars.' Or other times he would fetch one of the dining-room chairs and hold it up, cracking an imaginary whip. Either way, I always got tired before he did.

'I'm sorry,' I said gruffly.

Dad nodded. 'Now, do you want some toast or not?'

I stood up, stomped down the hallway and sat down cross-legged on the kitchen floor.

'You're going to sit there, are you?' he asked.

'Yes,' I said, and then I waited for him to say something that I could yell about. He didn't. Dad made me some toast and then he sat down next to me, stretching his long legs out over the linoleum and nursing a coffee cup.

'Who pays the bills?' I asked between bites.

He took a sip of his coffee. 'Why do you ask?'

'Well, I had a fight with Mum before, and I said she never did anything for us, it was all you, and she said, "Ask him who pays the bills."'

He put the cup on the floor and folded his hands in his lap. 'She does,' he said.

I chewed on my mouthful of toast. 'What, everything?' I asked.

'Pretty much.'

'Even for Kyle?'

Dad nodded.

'But Kyle refuses to see her,' I said.

'Whether he sees her or not – he's still her son.'

'What do you mean *everything*?'

'Well, she pays for your clothes, your school fees, your books, the light bill, the telephone.'

I held up the corner of my toast, looked at it and dropped it on the plate.

'What do you pay for?' I asked.

'I pay a portion too.'

'Less of a portion?'

Dad picked up my corner of toast and popped it in his mouth, brushing the crumbs from his fingers. 'Yes.'

'But what about the workshop?'

'The workshop has never been very profitable. It pays for itself.'

'But not very much?' I asked.

He shook his head. 'Not compared to your mother.'

I folded my arms and leaned my head back against the cupboard door. 'But don't you find it unmanliating?'

'You mean emasculating?'

'Yeah.'

Dad took another long sip of his coffee. 'No, I don't. When two people have babies, then two people are responsible for them as long as they live – and afterwards, although that seems to have gone out of fashion.'

He looked at me for a moment, and then he said, 'If I'd been the one doing the leaving, then I would probably be the one doing the paying, but as it is, we all live quite comfortably. Adele hasn't ever been stingy or grudging about it.'

'But don't you wish you could pay for us on your own? Don't you wish you didn't need her?'

'There are two answers to that,' he said. 'Firstly, when you decide to spend the rest of your life with someone then you go through a few ceremonies, some of them are formal, like a wedding, but another is less, shall we say, public. Making you and Kyle was a deliberate thing that your mother and I did together.'

I put my hands over my ears. 'Yuck, yuck. I don't want to know.'

He reached over and drew my hands away. 'No, you need to hear this, Bindy.'

I put my hands down and listened.

'We decided to make babies, and you are a great source of joy in a lot of ways, but one of them is that you are, and will always be, parts of me and parts of Adele all mingled together in a way that nobody can ever take apart. So, whether or not we are dependent on her financially, your mother and I are bound forever and ever by you two kids, and, in turn, by kids that you may have somewhere down the track, who will also be parts of me and parts of her. Do you get it?'

I nodded.

Dad stood up and took his cup and my plate to the sink.

'What was the other answer?' I asked.

He rinsed the crockery thoroughly and put them in the dishwasher, and then he squatted down in front of me.

'The second answer is this; you will make a number of momentous choices in your life. One is choosing between doing what you love most in the world, and doing what will make you wealthy. Some lucky people can get that with one job, but it's pretty rare.'

'So do you love panel-beating?'

Dad nodded.

'*Why?*' I asked, screwing up my nose.

He crossed his arms over his knees and leaned his chin on his wrist. 'When cars first arrive at the workshop they're broken and bent and scratched, and quite often – not all the time, but often enough – there has been a whole lot of pain and trauma associated with how they got to be that way. So me and the guys get out our dollies and we gently tap and shape and fill. Then we rub it down and we spray and by the time the vehicle leaves it's all shiny and new – so shiny and new that you'd never know it had ever happened.' He grinned. 'We're the cosmetic surgeons of the automotive industry.'

'You really love it?' I asked.

'Yes, I really love it.'

'So you reckon that it's better to do what you love?' I asked.

Dad stood up again and stretched from side-to-side.

'No, what I'm saying is that it's what I choose. When the time comes, you will have to decide that one for yourself.'

Then he leaned forward again, resting his hands on his knees. 'I'm saying that the fact that your mother is willing to support you – and me, to some degree – means that the choice for me is easy.'

When he first said that he was doing what he loved, I thought it sounded noble – as though he was pursuing a dream and wouldn't be swayed by greed; but when he put it like that, it almost sounded a little bit selfish.

Twenty-seven

Kyle came home from school and went into his room shutting the door behind him. I made us both a Milo, and then I tried Kyle's door, but it was locked.

'Hang on a minute,' he said. After a moment he opened the door a crack. 'What?' he asked. I tried to see past him into the room, but he closed the door a fraction, so that only his nose was visible.

'What are you doing?' I asked.

'Nothing. Are you OK? What do you want?'

'Have you got a girl in there with you?'

'No.'

'Let me see,' I said, pushing the door. Kyle held it firmly.

'I've got some news on the soccer jerseys,' I began.

'What?' he asked.

'I'm not telling until you let me in.'

'All right, all right,' he said and flung the door open. Spread out across the floor I could see around two dozen Micro Machines, Kyle's Furby and a scattering of Beast Wars dolls.

'Oh, so that's what you're up to – having a little play?'

'I was *cleaning* them. You have no idea how much a collection like this is worth in original condition.'

'Whatever you say, Kyle.' I paused. 'Cara told me how half your year came down to the quad today. And how everyone was going to fight everyone else.' I took a deep breath. 'Thanks for doing that.'

Kyle shook his head. 'I didn't have that much to do with it. Some of the girls in my year are pretty big on justice. They stood around in the common room, talking about how awful it was, getting all wound up about it, and then put together a little army.'

'Thanks anyway,' I said.

He bent down and picked up one of the Micro Machines. 'What's been happening here? Did Dad make you a comfort spud?'

I nodded. 'Liz rang. She said I should forgive Janey – not because what she did wasn't wrong, but because it would make it easier for everyone else if I just let it go.'

Kyle frowned. 'That sucks.'

'Yeah.'

'Liz has had a few heart-to-hearts with me recently. She's been coming in here and asking me about stuff – school and my hobbies.'

'Did you tell her about Furby, and your other toys?' I asked.

'They're figurines, and they're an *investment*.' He went on, 'It just seems a bit fake that's all – as though she has to get to know me – as if she's trying to *bond*.' He crossed his arms over his chest. 'So what's the big news?'

159

'There's some money for your jerseys already.'

Kyle moved some of the toys aside with his foot. 'How much?'

'A thousand dollars,' I replied.

Kyle's eyes lit up. 'Unreal, banana peel. Where from?'

'You really want to know?'

He shrugged. 'Yeah.'

'Mum.'

Kyle was still for a moment. His face was tight and angry. 'Who told her anyway? It was you, wasn't it?'

'Yes.'

He swore.

'You don't know what it's like,' I protested. 'Every time I see her it's "Kyle, Kyle, Kyle". What am I supposed to say?'

'You're supposed to say nothing. Thanks a million, Bindy.' He pushed passed me. 'I'm going to tell her. I'm going to tell her myself.'

Twenty-eight

Dad was in the workshop. The guys had gone for the day and he was sitting in his cramped, untidy office at the back making phone calls. I leaned against the door waiting for him to finish.

'How are you doing?' he asked, after he'd put the phone down.

'I'm fine,' I mumbled.

He looked down at the notes he made and then put his hand back on the phone. 'Do you want something? I can come inside in a minute and have a talk if you want, but I've got a few more calls that I'd like to make before five.' I scuffed my foot on the doorsill. It was covered in greasy bootprints.

'I've upset Kyle.'

'Really? And you've come to confess? My, you are a big girl now. What did you do – bang him over the head with the remote? Break his arm?'

I didn't look up.

'What is it?'

'Kyle's coaching the junior soccer team. He didn't tell you because he wants to do it on his own.' Then I explained to him about the jerseys, and the fund-raising competition, and how Mr Clemens thought it showed initiative. 'And I told Mum.'

Dad nodded. 'Let me guess. She offered to pay for them?'

'More than that – she's already given the money to the school. Kyle can't even turn it down.'

'Sneaky.' Dad's eyes narrowed. 'Can you hear that?'

'What?' I couldn't hear anything.

He shook his head slightly. 'Might be nothing. I'm sure Kyle will get over it.' He shuffled through the papers.

Kyle seemed pretty cross about it to me, and he wasn't all that good at forgiving either.

Dad put the papers down. 'Are you sure you can't hear anything? I think Kyle's in trouble.'

'So you're Lassie now?'

Dad smiled briefly. 'No, no, it's my spidey sense.' He was on his feet and striding towards the house.

As we opened the back door I could hear Kyle. He was yelling.

'No, I'm not grateful! You took it from me!'

Dad pushed the door open and rushed into the house. Kyle was in the kitchen shouting into the phone.

'I'm not being dramatic. You *stole* it. I don't care!'

He paused.

'I don't *want* you. You can't just buy everything. I'm not for sale!'

Kyle's face was red and I could see the veins raised on his throat. His eyes were glassy and he blinked rapidly, trying hard to keep from crying. He took a deep, gasping breath and his chest heaved.

'I *hate* you!'

He threw the phone towards the sink. It clattered across the draining board and there was a hollow crunching sound as it smashed a plate.

Dad stepped quickly across the room and threw his arms around Kyle. 'No!' Kyle struggled to get free.

Dad wouldn't let go. He had Kyle in a bear hug. 'Leave me alone,' yelled Kyle.

He flailed his arms around, and one of his hands clipped Dad in the side of the face. Dad's head whipped back for a second, but he tucked his chin down and hugged Kyle tighter.

'I *hate* her,' he said between gasps. 'She ruins *every-thing*.'

I stood in the doorway watching with my mouth open. Dad looked at me over Kyle's shoulder. He flicked his hand, signalling me to go away. I slunk behind the doorframe and peered around it.

Kyle's face was so red I thought it was going to burst. He let out another breath and his voice made a little squealing sound.

Dad put his hand on the back of Kyle's head. 'Let it go,' he said quietly.

Kyle collapsed against Dad's chest, letting out big racking sobs. He was taller than Dad, and he leaned against him with both hands clutching the front of

Dad's shirt. Dad was straining with the weight, and slipped one foot further out behind to brace himself.

Kyle cried as though years' worth of tears had been building up inside, like a big dam. I hadn't seen him cry since he was about twelve. And it was my fault. I'd told Mum about the jerseys, and at the time I hadn't been thinking about Kyle at all. I was the Milk Pig. Underneath Kyle's anguished voice I heard another voice coming from the lounge room. A few seconds later Liz peeked around the door. She was holding a box of her baked goodies.

'The door was open,' she explained.

Kyle sprang away from Dad and staggered back a few steps, slumping into one of the dining chairs.

Liz surveyed the scene. 'Kyle, are you all right?'

'He's a little bit upset,' replied Dad.

'Here,' she said, opening the box and holding it towards him. Kyle turned his face away from her, and then he stood up and stalked towards his bedroom, covering his face with his arm.

We all looked at each other. I was embarrassed. Liz wasn't supposed to see us like this – so raw.

'I'm sorry, John,' she said. 'I should have called first.'

Dad waved an arm at her. 'It's not your fault.' He paused. 'Give us a kiss, then.'

She stepped towards him and they kissed. I looked away.

'What's wrong with your face?' she asked.

He put his hand to his cheek where it had gone red. 'Kyle hit me,' he replied. 'He didn't mean to,' Dad added quickly. 'He was just reeling around the room, the way boys do when they're upset.'

'Janey does a bit of reeling around too, but I suppose you already know that.' She looked at me, and gave me a brief cheerless smile.

'Would you like to pop the kettle on? I'll just go and check on him.' Dad patted her forearm and then disappeared down the hallway.

'Where's Janey?' I asked.

Liz turned on the kettle and started picking up pieces of broken crockery out of the sink. 'She's at Hannah's. I've grounded her, but that seemed unfair, considering.'

'Considering what?' I asked.

Liz sighed. 'Hannah's family is moving overseas. She only found out for sure yesterday. Janey might not see her again, or at least for a long time, so I said she can start her grounding tomorrow.' She leaned against the sink. 'Janey's been suspended from school.'

I didn't care. In fact, I was glad.

'I'm not sad that Hannah's moving away,' Liz said quietly. She had the dishcloth in her hands and was folding it into a neat square.

'Me neither,' I replied.

When I looked at her face I remembered that before Hannah, Janey and her mum had been good friends. Liz had lost Janey because of Hannah too. I felt sorry for Liz, but that didn't stop me from being angry with Janey.

'Yeah, well, Janey doesn't need much encouragement to do the wrong thing,' I said, crossing my arms.

'Maybe, but she doesn't need much encouragement to do the right thing either,' Liz replied.

She moved over to the table and pushed the box of biscuits towards me. 'I actually brought these for you. They're bought ones, I'm afraid. I didn't have time to make up a batch myself. Sometimes when I've had a rough day I like to sit down to a nice box of bikkies.'

'Thanks,' I mumbled, reaching into the box.

'I've been eating an awful lot of bikkies recently,' she said, smiling and taking one herself.

Kyle and Dad came back out of his room and sat at the dining-room table. Liz finished making the coffee and set it on the table with the open box of goodies. Kyle's eyes were red, and he sniffed occasionally, but otherwise he seemed OK.

'What's this all about then?' asked Liz.

'Adele donated some money to the school for Kyle's junior soccer team,' Dad explained.

Kyle ran the back of his hand under his nose. 'She didn't even ask me. She wasn't supposed to know Bindy and I were going to do a fund-raiser. I was going to get the kids involved. I had it all planned out. They were suppose to . . . I don't want them to think that money just . . .' he trailed off. The whole time he was speaking he didn't look up from the table.

Liz patted his hand. 'I'm sure it's not as bad as it seems.'

Kyle glared at her – his mouth turned down at the sides as though he was going to cry again. Then he shoved his chair back from the table.

'This has got nothing to do with you. You think just because you're with Dad you've got a right to know my business, but you don't. So just back off!' Then he marched out of the room.

Liz watched him leave. Her hand nervously plucked at the tablecloth.

'He's just upset. He doesn't mean it,' Dad said, reaching across to her.

Everything was a mess. Nobody was happy. It was as though someone had shaken the rug under this family and every one of us would stumble around, coughing and sneezing until the dust had settled.

I stood up and walked into Kyle's room. He was sitting at his computer. I leaned against the desk, not saying anything.

'They would have been *proud* of those jerseys if they'd had to work for them. It would have made them a better team. Mum thinks getting out the chequebook is the solution to everything, but it wasn't about the money — not for me.'

He called her Mum. I wondered if he even noticed. He went on, 'Liz is never going to be our mum. She thinks she can just come in here and start solving our problems for us,' but we're *raised* already. We've done fine without her. It's not exactly as if she's done such a great job with Janey anyway.'

'She's trying to help.'

'I don't *want* her help. I didn't ask her. I don't want anybody's help. Yours either, so can you please just go?' He slumped over the desk with his forehead in the crook of his elbow

I rubbed my forehead. Going would be fantastic. It would have been great to walk out the door and leave the whole mess behind, but where was I going to go *to*?

'Liz might be as hopeless as the other two, but I don't think she's mean,' I said.

Kyle rubbed his face in his hands. 'I just wish you'd all leave me alone.'

Dad and Liz peered around the doorframe as if on cue.

'Son?' said Dad quietly – whispering as though he was approaching a sleeping dragon. 'We've had an idea.'

'We'll have a cake stall,' said Liz.

'Liz can do some of her great biscuits,' said Dad.

'All the soccer kids can help make up the batter, so they'll be involved – like you said,' added Liz.

Kyle groaned. He leaned forward and banged his head on the edge of the desk.

Twenty-nine

The next morning when I woke up I noticed a note on the kitchen bench.

Staying with Liz. Don't go to school if you don't feel like it. Otherwise ride your bike. Dad.

When I flipped the notebook over I saw another message on the page before.

Just popped over to Liz's. Might be back. If not, you can call me there. Dad.

And the page before that.

Going to Liz's. Probably be back before you wake up. Any problems, you know the number. Dad.

He'd been staying over at Liz's place and I hadn't even noticed. Janey was right. He *was* spending all his time with Liz. What if something had happened while he was away? What if there had been burglars, or crazed murderers? How would he feel if he came home and found us dead in our beds?

Imagine all the stuff Janey could get away with if Dad and Liz weren't here to stop her? The Undies Incident would be just the beginning.

I sprawled out on the lounge and turned on the telly. I stayed there all day, flipping from channel to channel. I ate all of Liz's biscuits. I even had a little nap.

At around five o'clock there was a knock at the door and I went to answer it.

'Mum!'

She was standing on the doorstep with her arms folded looking out at the street. She turned to look at me.

'Kyle's not home yet,' I said.

'I'm not here for Kyle. He's a bit grumpy with me at the moment.'

A bit grumpy? Yes, and Queen Elizabeth has a bit of an English accent.

'I want to show you something. Is it all right if you come over tonight? I can drop you at school in the morning.'

'I suppose so. I'll just go and check with Dad.'

Dad said it was fine, but I think he was as perplexed as I was. She'd never invited me on a school night before. She was up to something.

When Mum pulled into her car space at the apartment I noticed that there was another car parked in front of it – a BMW four-wheel drive, and worse still, in *gold*. It had a matching designer shovel on the back, but at least it didn't have a snorkel.

'Whose is that?' I asked.

'Phillip's,' she answered.

I snorted. 'That'd be right.' I hadn't realised just how easy Phillip was going to make it for me to find things to hate about him.

Mum didn't comment.

Upstairs, the door opened, and there was the man himself. Phillip was wearing a linen shirt with some kind of brand name on it, beige linen pants and tasselled slip-on shoes. He looked like he might be a bit of a goose. Then he said, *'Buenos días, muchacha,'* even though he wasn't Spanish, and it was clear that he *was* a goose – a great, big, logo-wearing, tosser-car-driving, Spanish-speaking goose.

'Hi,' I said.

'This is Phillip,' said Mum, smiling.

'Yeah, I figured that out for myself,' I said.

Mum took a deep breath. 'Phillip has made us a nice dinner.'

'Coq au vin. My speciality,' he said.

Fantastic. It's going to be one big European adventure tonight, I can just tell.

'But first I want to show you something,' she said, taking me by the hand and leading me down the hall-way. She turned the study door handle with a flourish and it swung open. 'Ta da!' She stood there with her arm out and smiling, like a game-show, gift-shop girl.

I dropped my bag to the floor.

The whole room, carpet to ceiling, was periwinkle blue. There was a huge bed and on it a blue doona cover sprinkled with little white stars. There was a desk in the corner near the window with a computer on it.

On the bedside table was lamp and beside it a photo frame, the picture of Mum and me at Wonderland, taken by Barney Rubble.

'Wow, Mum. This looks great,' I said.

'You like it?' she asked. 'When you were little I had your room painted green. I remember when you first saw it you were so disappointed. You said you wished it were blue.'

'I don't remember that.'

'You cried, and I . . . I was hoping that maybe this time I would get it right.'

I felt a little prickle of tears in my eyes. Mum saw it too. She looked away from me, pointing to a poster on the wall that I hadn't noticed. 'I got this picture of Britney, but I wasn't sure if you liked her,' she said. 'We can change it.'

'Actually, that's Jessica Simpson,' I said.

'Oh,' she replied. 'Do you like her?'

'Mmm,' I said. 'I just love the curtains!'

They were dark blue with little stars like the bedspread.

'So this is OK?' she asked.

'It's gorgeous, Mum. Thank you, but you shouldn't have gone to all this trouble, I mean, we're hardly ever here, are we?'

Mum sat down on the edge of the bed. 'Well, actually, chicken . . .' she began.

Oh no. I could see it. I could see her grand plan stretched out in front of me.

'Phillip and I have been talking, and we think we're probably in a better position than your father to accommodate your needs. Especially if he is starting a new relationship.'

I quickly looked away.

'We're certainly more central,' she continued. 'We can even take you out of that school if you want to. There's a girls' college only a few blocks away. You could walk to school. They have an excellent reputation, and the uniforms are *very* flattering. I've brought home some brochures.'

Another school. At a new school no one would know that I was the Whistle Farter. They wouldn't have ever seen my cottontails either.

'I know this must be a surprise for you, and I'm sure you've got a lot to think about. How about you just have a little sit in here, and get the feel of it, while I go and see how dinner is coming along?' She patted me on the knee and then she left, closing the door behind her.

At a new school I could start again. No Janey. No history at all. I could leave all the horribleness behind and be a whole brand-new person that had never existed before.

I stood up and walked across the room — the new spacious room that I wouldn't ever have to share with anybody — opened the sliding doors out onto the terrace. Putting my hands on the railing, I looked out across the fairy lights of the houses in the valley.

Thirty

There was, of course, one big fat downside to this whole plan.

'Here we go *ma chérie*,' Phillip said, placing the plate in front of me. It smelt good, if you're into big chunks of bird, and vegetables with all the life boiled out of them. 'So, has your mother told you about *la idea*?'

'Yep.'

'And what do you think?' he asked, smoothing a serviette across his lap.

We never used serviettes at Dad's. He just told us to wash our hands, or failing that, he rubbed our faces with a teatowel.

'What do you think of *das Schlafzimmer*?' he asked.

'I'm sorry?'

'The bedroom,' Mum said. 'Phillip is multi-lingual.' She reached across the table and squeezed his hand.

'No kidding,' I said.

Phillip broke off a piece of bread and watched me while he chewed. 'So, Bindy, Adele tells me you're quite the science whiz.'

Mum thought I was smart because she'd told me so often that now she believed it. I wasn't a 'whiz' at anything. I didn't do badly at school, but she wasn't really in a position to know either way.

'Have you had a chance to look at the computer in there? Are you into computers at all? It's quite a good one. I built it myself a few months ago but I find I use the laptop more. Do you use computers at school yet? That girls' college down the road. What's it called, Darling?' He turned to Mum and then went on. 'They have computers in all the classrooms. Very impressive. We did a tour of the grounds earlier this week. How do you feel about going there?'

'I . . .'

He sawed at his chicken. 'We think you'll love it.'

'May I have a drink of water?' I asked.

'Help yourself,' Mum said.

I left the table. From the kitchen I could hear them whispering.

'I think you might be coming on a bit strong,' Mum said.

'You think?' he asked.

'Let's just take it slowly.'

I stood at the kitchen sink and drank a whole glass of water in one long gulp. I really wanted to hate Phillip, and he was certainly giving me lots of opportunities, but I also felt guilty about it. It wasn't voluntary. Somehow it was much easier to hate from a distance than it was face-to-face.

As I sat back down again they both beamed at me.

175

'Did you know you can walk to the beach from here?' Phillip began. 'There is a charity swim each year from bluff to bluff. I've done it the last few years. It's absolutely exhausting. I've never broken any records, but it's not about that, is it? What's that saying? "The greatest test of courage on earth is to bear defeat without losing heart."'

'"The moment of victory is much too short to live for that and nothing else,"' I added.

'Who said that? Socrates?' Phillip asked.

I shook my head. 'Martina Navratilova.'

'So you like tennis?' he asked.

'We had to do an assignment on a famous sportsperson in Studies in Society,' I explained.

'Great. Great,' he said, nodding. Phillip crossed his knife and fork and pushed his plate away. There was a long awkward silence. I could feel he was building to something.

'Bindy, I know we've only just met, but your mother and I have been talking, and the more we talked about it the more excited I got about it. Really.'

He reached across and grabbed Mum's hand.

I looked down at my plate. 'Thanks for dinner. It was nice.'

'A few of the ladies have brought me some books on parenting. I haven't read them yet, but I will.'

He sounded like he was preparing for a project.

I turned to Mum. 'Have you talked to Dad about this?'

'Your mother tells me that John is a great father,' Phillip said. 'I'm sure he's terrific.'

Right. That's enough. I shoved my chair back from the table. 'May I be excused?'

'Of course, chicken,' Mum said.

I picked up my plate and carried it to the kitchen. My head was spinning and I was sure that any minute I would keel over.

Back in the dining room I overheard Phillip speaking in a low voice to my mother. 'She's got great table manners, Adele. I was surprised, I mean, we could take her out anywhere.'

I walked to my room and closed the door quietly behind me. I grabbed one of the pillows and curled around it on the bed. Right in front of me was the Wonderland picture. Somewhere along the way, and I have no idea when this happened, I had grown to the same height as my mother. We were both grinning and laughing as though we were having the time of our lives, but I remembered that day quite vividly. I didn't want to be there.

The door opened quietly and Mum came and sat on the edge of the bed.

'Belinda, I don't want to press you, but maybe you could give me some idea of what you're thinking.'

I shifted over towards the wall.

'Either way is fine,' she went on. 'If you don't want this, then just say so. But I want to make it clear to you just how committed Phillip and I are.'

'Do I have to answer right now?' I asked.

Mum ran her hand along the edge of the bedspread picking at invisible lint and loose threads. 'No, but what's your gut reaction?'

My gut reaction is no. Wait a second. Maybe it's yes? I don't know

'I don't know, Mum. This is never something I've ever thought about before.'

Mum flicked and picked relentlessly at the hem. I wanted to grab her hands and push them away. *Just give it a rest, will you?*

'Do I have to go to school tomorrow? I mean, if I did agree to come here and live with you, could I start at the new school straight away?'

'Well, of course you would have to keep going to your old school for a little while. You'd probably start at the new school next term.'

I snorted. Next term? Next term was a million years away!

Then she turned on me. 'What? What is it that I'm doing wrong? You tell me, Belinda, because I've tried to anticipate every single thing that you might need here. What are you looking for?'

I sat up. 'Why can't you stop trying to guess what will make me happy all the time, and just *ask* me?'

We stared at each other.

She folded her arms. 'OK, fine. What will make you happy?'

I opened my mouth and then shut it again. 'I don't know yet. I need to think it through.'

She stood up. 'You're just impossible. You know that? You're just like your father — so bloody indecisive!'

'What are you doing this for?' I yelled at her. 'Why

now? You've had years and years, and all of a sudden you want an answer this second!'

Her face screwed up and her lips narrowed. 'I don't want Little-Missus-Handy-Home-Hints within ten miles of you, or your brother. She has no right!'

Then she strode out, flinging the door closed behind her.

Thirty-one

I lay on the bed with my brain in a knot. Why did it have to be so complicated? Mum was always trying to make me do what she wanted. Dad left me alone. Right at that moment I was cranky with both of them in equal proportions.

In a perfect world I would live here, but with Dad and Kyle. Mum could visit us on weekends, but she would be pleasant and bake cookies, and not try to run our lives. But this isn't a perfect world. There was no third option. I had to choose.

Maybe someone else could choose for me? I looked at the phone. Who could tell me what to do?

I picked up the handset and rang home. I could talk to Kyle. He would tell me I was crazy to even consider it, but that was fine. That was a decision.

It rang a few times and then a voice answered. 'Hello?' I said.

'Oh, hi, Bindy. Are you OK?' It was Little-Missus-Handy-Home-Hints herself.

'Yeah,' I said. 'I'm . . .'

And then it occurred to me that perhaps I could talk to Liz. On impulse, I blurted, 'Mum has asked me to move in with her.'

Liz paused. 'And how do you feel about that?'

I wound the phone cord around my finger, already regretting that I'd said anything. 'I'm not sure.'

'Well, that's a tough one. We'd all miss you so much. And your father . . .' She took a deep breath. 'Oh Bindy, there's always been a sort of silent tug-of-war for you, hasn't there?'

'Kind of,' I mumbled.

When Liz started talking again, she sounded as tentative as I was – as though she was in the dark and slowly feeling her way. 'Your mum is . . . How shall I put this? She'll always want what she thinks is best for you, but that can vary.'

'Yeah,' I said. 'I've won a few battles recently, and she's trying.'

'Good for you!'

There was an awkward pause and I felt so stupid for raising the whole thing with her.

After a moment she started talking again. 'There's so much happening in all our lives at the moment. If you make decisions based on what has happened in the last few days, you might find that next week everything is different again. Do you know what I mean? Perhaps you should just concentrate on being Bindy, and ignore everything else.'

'Mmm.'

She paused again. 'I'm sorry, Bindy, I haven't been much help.'

'No, you've been helpful. I hadn't thought of it that way. I was really thinking about which one would get me off the most school.'

She laughed.

I was about to hang up.

'Oh and Bindy?' she started.

'Yeah?'

'I don't like to meddle when it comes to you two girls, but Janey's been crying all afternoon. She feels bad about what happened at school. She tells me that there's some gang of older girls after her, but I'm sure she's exaggerating. I just wanted you to know that she's worried about you and she seems genuinely sorry.'

'Yeah, OK.'

After I hung up the phone, I changed into my jammies and climbed into the giant bed.

The girl who would live in this house with Adele and Phillip, and attend a girls' college down the road would be a different Bindy altogether. She would have excellent table manners and speak confidently with her elders about various community charity events, and after a while, she might start having 'key priorities'.

That Bindy might not ever fart in public, or have the whole world see her undies, but neither would she have Cara, James, Kyle and even Janey, around her every day to make her realise that it really wasn't that big a deal.

Thirty-two

When I came out to the kitchen the next morning, Mum had attempted to make pancakes and all the benches were a mess of flour and eggshells.

'You can get this stuff in a bottle now,' she said to me, plonking a plate in front of me. 'Or ready-made. You just pop them in the toaster. I think I'll do that next time.'

'I usually just have a piece of toast,' I said.

She stood with her back to me. 'I've decided I'm not going to pressure you any more, chicken,' she continued. 'I'm just going let you tell me when you're ready. OK?'

'OK,' I sat down again.

'Would you like me to braid your hair?' she asked.

Not really, but I could see that *she* wanted to braid my hair. Besides, if it looked bad I could always take it out later.

'If you like.' I shrugged.

She stood behind me and ran her fingers through my hair, dividing it into equal parts.

'Mum?'

'Yes, honey?'

'Dad told me about how you pay for everything.'

She didn't say anything.

'I just wanted to say thanks. That's all.'

'I'm glad you appreciate it.' She gave my hair a sharp tug and then tied it off. 'There you go. All done.'

Mum made coffee and we sat opposite each other at the table.

After a long and uncomfortable silence, Mum leaned back and crossed her legs. 'You're not going to come and live with us, are you?'

I shook my head.

There. It was out. It was done. That wasn't so bad, was it?

Mum's face went all wonky for a second and then she composed herself. 'Can I ask why not?'

I stared down at my plate. 'I don't think it's the best thing for me right now.'

She crossed her arms. 'And that's your final decision, is it?'

'I don't think it should have to be final,' I said quietly.

After an icy drive, I stood outside the school. Students streamed off buses and around me through the gates. I didn't want to go in.

Looking past the teachers' carpark I could see the quadrangle and the dais where I had stood while the whole school passed around my undies. The memory of it washed over me and made me cringe.

The last thing I needed was another day of having to be strong and handle the comments that people made.

For them it was just a way of drawing attention to themselves, and trying to be cool in front of their friends – they might even think they were saying something nice. For me it was another situation that I had no control over, and that I had to hunker down and weather, until the next crisis came along. I was too tired for that.

I decided not to go in. I needed another day – I needed a week, but a day would do.

Just as I turned around to start the long walk home, I heard a voice. 'Hey, Bindy!'

It was Cara. I looked back and saw her standing at the edge of the quad waving. She had a big goofy grin on her face. James was with her, and together they ran towards me.

'We've been waiting for you.'

'We missed you yesterday.'

'Are you OK?'

When they reached me, they each linked their arms in mine, like a pair of crutches, and led me along the path and into the school.

'Yeah, I'm OK,' I said, smiling.

All day they sat on either side of me – two human shields. A few of the boys made some jokes in class, but when they did, other people – even people I didn't know very well – told them not to be so slack.

In Science we were given a group assignment to do and the three of us agreed to do it together. We decided to meet up at my place the following week to start work on it, and even though it was schoolwork, I was looking forward to it.

When the bell rang at the end of the day I sighed. I had made it through this day. It hadn't been so bad.

Thirty-three

Mr Clemens was not at all opposed to the idea of us raising extra funds for the Junior Soccer Team and even gave us permission to use one of the cooking rooms during the weekend.

Dad and Liz bustled around with matching aprons. Janey sat in the corner with her arms folded and a sour look on her face. Kyle was really anxious at first but his little soccer kiddies were so exuberant that he really had his hands full, and after a while he started laughing and having a good time. The parents dropped them off, and then stayed for a while, helping make sure that more of the chocolate went into the cookies than into the Junior Soccer Team's mouths.

Cara and James came too. We had a great flour fight until Liz got cross with us and told us we were setting a bad example. She sent us to sit outside.

We lay on the grass listening to the kids yelling and enjoying the biscuit smells wafting out through the window. I pulled out some grass and twiddled it between my fingers.

'Janey's having fun,' James said.

Cara rolled over onto her stomach. 'So what did she do?'

'What are you talking about?' I asked.

'That day when you were fighting you said you didn't dob. What did she do?'

I shook my head. 'I'm not telling.'

Cara snorted and rolled on her back. 'Not fair!'

James folded his legs, wrapping his arms around his calves. He was looking particularly handsome, with his hair glossy and clean. 'You want to hear the worst thing I ever did?'

'Yeah,' said Cara, sitting up.

'One time – I was probably about six or seven, I can't really remember – my mum took me Christmas shopping. She gave me that whole story about how she was helping Santa out. She was stressed, the way parents are around Christmas time, and we'd been out for hours. We were in one of the department stores, and the toy section was next to menswear or something. She was buying stuff and I wandered off. I found one of those Power Rangers figurines and I really wanted it. I had a jumper with me. Mum always makes me take a jumper everywhere, just in case. As if there's going to be a sudden cold snap on Christmas Eve, but that's my mum. She must have been a Scoutmaster in a former life. Anyway, I had this jumper so I wrapped the figurine in it and tucked it under my arm, trying to look casual. When I turned around, Santa was standing there at the end of the aisle.'

'Did he see you?' asked Cara.

'Santa bent over, right up close to me, and he said, "Have you been a good little boy?"'

'What did you do?' I asked.

'I freaked out. I screamed and I ran away crying,' he said, smiling. I'd never noticed what great teeth he had. So straight.

'What about the Power Ranger doll?' Cara asked.

'Figurine,' James corrected. 'I've still got it somewhere, I think.'

'So he didn't see you?' she said.

James shrugged. 'If he did, he didn't say anything. And I still got all my presents, so I guess he forgave me.'

'Would you do it again?' I asked.

James shook his head. 'No way, man.'

'But you got away with it,' I said.

'Not really,' he said, shaking his head. 'I never played with that figurine. If Mum saw me with it she'd want to know where it came from, so I had to keep it secret.

'I could never really relax with it. Every time I brought it out, all I could see was Santa's big ruddy face right in front of mine. I don't want to own any more stuff that makes me feel like that.'

'What about you, Cara?' I asked.

She shrugged. 'I've stolen money from my mum's purse.'

'What have *you* done?' James asked me.

'Oh, I've done some bad things,' I replied.

He sat up straight. 'What? Tell me!' The whites of his eyes were really white — almost blue.

189

I shook my head. The only bad things I'd ever done were Janey's idea. If I told them, then I'd be telling her secrets. 'Maybe some other time.'

'Go on!' said Cara.

'I'm not going to tell you,' I said.

Cara stood up, wiping her hands on the bum of her jeans. 'Back in a minnie,' she said.

James watched her walk away through the door and then he scooted over closer to me.

'Bindy, I ...' he started. 'Do you think you might want to, like, kiss, maybe ... now?'

I lay there on my back, frozen, my heart ka-thumping in my chest, and my skin prickling. This was it. He was going to kiss me. I wanted him to, but at the same time I wanted to run away.

'Umm, yeah, OK,' I stammered.

He leaned over – his face moving closer and closer to mine until I could see the pores on his skin. My whole body shivered with goose-bumps and then I shut my eyes.

His lips clamped down over my mouth, wider than I had anticipated, like a plumbing seal. I tried to compensate by opening my mouth a little, but he just widened his more, like a big suck-face. He poked his tongue out and it bumped against mine and slid to the side. He tasted like biscuit dough. I opened my eyes and turned my face away. 'I don't know if I'm ready for this,' I said.

'What do you mean?'

'Well, I think I'm supposed to be concentrating on my feelings for you, and stuff like that, but I'm sort of focused on the mechanics.'

'Oh,' he said.

'It's just . . . well, it's not very romantic. I expected that it would all go smoothly, like it does in the movies.'

He blinked. 'How do you know people in the movies aren't concentrating on mechanics too?' He leaned close to me again. 'We just need to practise.'

I pulled back. 'No, James.'

He rolled on his back. 'I don't want to be your boyfriend any more,' he said grumpily. He looked up at the sky. 'It sounds like we're breaking up, doesn't it? Did I break up with you or did you break up with me?'

'James,' I said, 'we were never Going Out in the first place.'

'Yes, that's right.' He brushed his hands together.

We sat silently for ages.

'Do you think we can still be friends?' James asked. 'I really hope so, because I like hanging out with you, and Cara too.' He paused. 'Maybe next year you'll want to Go Out with me? Do you think you will?'

I smiled. 'The greatest test of courage is to bear defeat without losing heart,' I said.

'What?' he asked.

'Oh nothing.'

Thirty-four

The cake stall raised four hundred and fifty dollars – less than the five hundred and ten that Kyle would have needed for the jerseys. With Mum's money he had enough left over to repair the nets as well.

Hannah left for Malaysia. Janey cried. The day she came back to school after her suspension, Cara, James and I watched her doing laps of the perimeter fence, during recess from our place outside B Block. She looked nervous and stayed close to the front office. There was a ripple of expectation in the quad as if the whole school was waiting for the Year 11 girls to rush out in the quad.

'Can I rescue her?' asked James. 'Please?'

'You guys made me sit here by myself for ages!' I protested.

'You could have put your hand up. You were too proud,' he replied. 'So, can I?'

Cara and I exchanged a glance. I shrugged. 'Yeah,' why not?'

James cupped his hands around his mouth. 'Hey,

Janey.' She began to walk towards us. 'Want to join my harem?' he finished.

Janey hesitated – half a smile on her face. Cara slapped his arm.

I patted the grass beside me. 'Don't worry about him, he's just desperate.'

'Thanks,' she said, and sat down.

'No probs,' I replied.

Lots of heads turned our way and a few of the boys casually wandered over towards us. They were all hoping for a fight. After a while they lost interest and returned to their games.

We sat silently for a minute and then Cara stood up brushing the grass from the back of her skirt.

'James, do you want to come to the canteen with me?'

'Nah,' he said.

'Yes, you do,' she said, hauling at his arm.

'No, I don't,' he replied, resisting.

'I think you do, James,' I said.

He looked at me and then his eyes flicked towards Janey. 'Oh. OK.' Then he stood up.

Janey watched them walking down the path. 'That was nice of her,' she said.

I nodded. 'Cara's good like that.'

She stared straight ahead. 'Sorry about the thing with the undies.'

I stretched my legs out and leaned back on my palms. 'I'll live.'

'It wasn't my idea,' she said. 'I didn't know what they

were going to do. Well, I knew, but Hannah was only supposed to take one pair, and Mitchell was meant to wear them on his head, like a hat, in Science, and then we were going to give them straight back to you. I didn't realise that they had taken so many, or that they would do it in front of the whole school.'

Oh yes, that plan was much less humiliating – and so *mature*.

'Forget it, OK?'

'No, Bindy, I'm *really* sorry.' She paused for a moment, looking at the ground. 'So is it truly OK if I sit with you guys?'

'It's fine with me, Janey, but you might find that we're not on your level.'

She leaned over and punched me in the leg. 'Shut *up*.'

I laughed at her and she blushed.

Later that night, Janey and I were in Kyle's room playing *Battlefield*. Kyle and Janey had decided to act as if they'd never kissed. Sometimes pretendings come in handy.

Kyle was wearing the long-sleeved shirt that Mum bought for him.

We'd been playing so long that I didn't notice how late it was. It was almost three in the morning before I ventured out to make us all something to eat.

As I headed down the hall I didn't bother to turn the lights on – my eyes had adjusted to the dark. Besides I could see into the kitchen because there was a narrow wedge of light coming from the refrigerator.

I knelt down and watched. I don't know why I did

that. Maybe it was because I'd spent the last half an hour being a sniper, crawling across a virtual combat zone on my digital belly? It was Dad. I could see his mad-professor sleep hair poking out at the sides.

When I realised what he was doing, I scuttled back to Kyle's room to get the others.

'You've got to see this,' I whispered.

'What?' Janey asked.

I put my finger to my lips and motioned for them to follow me and they both scampered behind me into the hallway. Halfway down the hall, I switched the light on. There was Dad standing in the middle of the kitchen, a two-litre bottle of milk to his lips and an open tin of Milo on the bench.

When the light came on, he pulled the bottle down so fast it sloshed out and onto his T shirt, leaving a muddy brown stain.

'Milk Pig!' I shouted, pointing at him.

'Am not!' he protested, with the bottle still in his hand, label side out, as though he was in an ad.

'Dad, you have a milk *moustache*!' I said.

'You're busted like custard!' added Kyle.

'What are you doing up anyway? It's way past your bedtime,' he said.

Janey butted in. 'All this time we've been blaming each other and it was you!'

Dad looked over her shoulder and pointed. 'Look, behind you! Elephant!'

Janey looked over her shoulder, but Kyle and I didn't. It was an old joke. Dad grabbed the tin of Milo and his milk, and bounded through his bedroom door, slamming it behind him.

We all stared at each other. I was about to say something when Dad opened the door again and poked out his head.

'Don't you girls go giving Kyle any of that dope of yours,' he said, and then he slammed the door again.

Kyle stared at me. 'What was *that* about?'

Janey's mouth dropped open. 'You!' she said, pointing at me.

I shook my head. 'I didn't dob, Janey, I swear!'

'You absolutely swear?'

'Honest, Janey. I never said anything!'

'Are you a *druggo*?' asked Kyle, surprised.

'As if!' protested Janey.

Later that night Janey and I were in our room. I thought she was asleep on the trundle, but then she spoke. 'Do you reckon John really knows about me smoking?' she whispered.

'Yeah, of course he does.'

'But if he knows, then how come I didn't get into trouble?'

I tucked my hands behind my head. 'He doesn't operate like that. If he says we're not allowed to do something, then it will just make us do it behind his back, but if he lets us know that he knows, then it's up to us to make the choice.'

I could hear her rolling over. 'That's dumb. How do you know? Maybe he's actually saying it's OK.'

'I just know.'

I also knew that when he said 'you girls', what he really meant was 'Janey'. If he even suspected that it had been me, he would have given me a stern talking-to.

She sat up. 'But how do you know he's thinking that?'

I smiled. 'Well, Janey, maybe it's because I'm just more mature than you.'

A pillow flew out of the darkness and hit me in the face.

I wrestled it away. 'See? This is exactly the kind of thing I'm talking about.'